Return of the Highland Laird

A Novella
~Book Four: Highland Force Series~

by

Amy Jarecki

Rapture Books

Copyright © 2014, Amy Jarecki

Jarecki, Amy
Return of the Highland Laird

Paperback ISBN: 9781942442462
Alternative ISBN: 978-0692248065

First Release: August, 2014

Book Cover Design by: Kim Killion

To Christine and Caroll, the best critique partners a girl could have!

Chapter One

The North Channel, off the coast of Scotland, March, 1587

The gale hit with destructive force as Alexander's small *birlinn* rounded the Mull of Galloway and sailed into the Irish Sea. With a crack, the rope steadying the rudder snapped and whipped through the air, smacking him across the face with the power of a bullwhip. Clapping a hand to his bloody cheek, Alexander reeled back. A gust of wind blasted in from the starboard side. His grip slipped from the sail line. He tightened his fist, but the hemp rope cut through his palm like a slicing dagger.

His wounds stung, but if he wanted to live, he'd best fight the sea.

The square sail collapsed and flapped, resembling bed linens hung out in a storm. Angry white swells crashed over the bow and the boat listed from side to side. If he didn't gain control soon, the *birlinn* would capsize for certain. The boom groaned and swung toward him with deadly speed. Alexander ducked and dove for the rudder.

Slippery from the driving rain, he steadied the long oaken handle under his arm. It took all his strength to keep the boat on course. Peering over the bow, he could see nothing but rain and waves so high they could swallow him into the icy depths at any moment. Though late afternoon, the clouds dominated the sky, making it dark as midnight.

A lightning bolt flashed and streaked into three fingers, followed immediately by a deafening roll of thunder.

His heart pummeling his chest, Alexander planted his feet against a rowing bench and pulled back with all his strength, roaring with the agony of exertion. The boat listed portside. Alex countered with the rudder. Rain and saltwater funneled into his eyes, but he could spare not a heartbeat to wipe them.

On and on he fought the sea, damning himself to hell while lightning streaked and thunder boomed above. He'd been a fool to sail from Raasay alone. He'd been a fool in so many ways. He had no right to be laird of Clan MacLeod. If only he'd been the one who'd fallen from the curtain wall and not Ilysa. She'd never done anything to incite the wrath of God. But Alexander had. He deserved punishment worse than death.

A rogue wave crashed from the starboard side. Timbers cracked. The boat listed so far to port, Alexander clung to the rudder and closed his eyes. *Have mercy on my soul.*

With his next breath, the *birlinn* buoyed upright. Alex squinted through the rain. A light flickered in the distance. He blinked and it was gone, hidden by the deluge and enormous swells. Had he been mistaken? He hoped to God he hadn't and bore down on the rudder, praying his course was sound and the shore was near.

Though a robust man, every muscle burned while he fought the powerful current. The *birlinn* had twisted and turned so much, he could very well be on a course to the open sea—a folly no skilled sailor would ever make. If his father, the great Laird Calum MacLeod, were to see him now, he'd shake his head and turn away. Alexander had once thought he could follow in the wake of his father's success, but he'd failed.

Miserably.

His entire life, tragedy and destruction rained down upon him akin to the tempest now threatening each breath.

Ahead the light flickered again. Alexander's every muscle trembled with fatigue while he strained to see it. Brighter now, he spotted the glint each time the movement of the waves dipped. The *birlinn* bobbed with the sea and thrashed erratically. Alexander licked the salty sea water from his lips and strained to make out the shore. Sailing into rocks or cliffs would tear the boat into splinters. But the unrelenting rain refused to pause.

He kept the *birlinn* on course, convinced the light was a beacon calling to him. And then he saw it. The grey sands of a beach lay ahead, and yonder, a large whitewashed building—an inn for certain. Praise the heavens. He held fast to the rudder and set the course straight for the sand. When the boat skidded to a stop, Alex dropped anchor and jumped over the side into thigh-deep waves. The icy water was no colder than the plaid and shirt that clung to his skin.

The wind cut through him while he marched through the surf. Adjusting his sword belt, he ran his fingers over his dirk. He still didn't have his bearings. If the *birlinn* had sailed due south, he'd be on English soil. The thought made a shudder slither up his spine.

***

Jane battened the window shutter with a cross-board and turned to face Mr. Cox. "Please have a seat whilst you wait out this nasty squall."

"Thank you, my lady." The elderly man slid onto a bench at the table. "I haven't any idea where this downpour came from. There wasn't a cloud in the sky when I set out."

"I suppose 'tis the way of things in spring." She placed bowl on the floor to catch yet another dripping leak. "Soon it will be nice enough to mend the roof."

"I wish we could hire a laborer for the task."

"But we cannot." She reached for a ewer—at least the rain slapping upon the roof drowned out the water dripping into the pails and bowls strewn throughout the cottage. "Will you have a cup of watered wine while you wait?"

"My thanks." He sucked in a sharp inhale while she filled his cup. "It pains me to watch you serve me with your own fine-boned hand, Lady Whitehaven."

A familiar twinge of pain tugged her heartstrings. "You must stop calling me that."

"Why?" Mr. Cox made a show of casting his gaze around the tiny cottage. "No one will overhear us hidden so deep in the wood."

She poured for herself and sat. "True. Especially now the priory's closed."

"Disgraceful Reformation."

Jane smoothed her fingers over the cross pendant she wore. "At least things have settled since Queen Elizabeth sanctioned the Church of England."

Mr. Cox sipped. "Yes. If only the bloodshed would stop, along with the constant hunt for heretics."

"We must conform. 'Tis the only way." She forced herself to smile. "What news of Buttermere Castle?"

"I'm surprised you care, my lady."

She cast her gaze to the Whitehaven crest above the mantel—the one thing in the cottage that reminded her she once lived a life of privilege. "But I do care very much. I reigned as countess within its walls for eight years."

Mr. Cox's jowls jostled when he shook his head. "Miserable years they were, I'll say."

"Not entirely bad. Occasionally Roderick would travel to London, and I would have peace."

He raised his wooden cup in toast. "I cannot believe how you always choose to remember the good."

"Alas, the bad times are far too painful to speak of." She reached for a plate of kettle scones, pushing memories of beatings back to the locked recesses of her mind. "Tell me, how is the new Earl of Whitehaven settling in?"

"John Drake is not much better than your Roderick. I'm afraid the entire line of Whitehaven earls is spun of the same tainted cloth."

Jane clasped her hands to her stomach. The mere thought of the callous family she'd married into made her stomach clench like a stone. She jumped at a surge of rainwater splashing from the eaves. Thunder rumbled overhead, putting her further on edge. "If that is the case, I shall pray he remains unmarried."

Mr. Cox frowned and studied his boots. "God forbid another woman would suffer at the hands of the Earl of Whitehaven as did you, my lady."

Jane stood and crossed to the hearth, staring at the accursed family crest. "I cannot bring myself to think of it." She flicked her long tresses back and used an iron ladle to stir the pottage. True, for the past few months life had grown lonely—a tad tedious, even, but she would choose this reclusive existence over her past. She pushed the articulating arm to situate the cast iron pot closer to the flame. "How are the servants?"

"Same as always."

She stirred with more vigor. "In good health?"

"Yes, aside from Thomas. Sometimes the farrier doesn't know when to keep his opinions to himself. Lord Drake had him whipped but two days ago."

Jane stopped stirring, though she kept her face turned away. *More beatings? Did my sacrifice do nothing to bring them peace?* "I am sorry." Her voice trembled. "Is it bad?"

"He'll recover in a sennight or two." Mr. Cox didn't sound as convincing as his words.

Her heart twisted. She loved the servants, of whom she'd grown ever so fond at Buttermere. "If there were only something more I could do."

"But you cannot, must not."

She hadn't brought it up in some time, but with the news of renewed brutality, she had to ask. "Are the townsfolk still blaming me?" She regarded Mr. Cox over her shoulder.

The kindhearted valet had withered in the years she'd known him. His careworn face paled. "Now more than ever, I'm afraid. Lord Whitehaven has increased the bounty for your capture—says you're a murderess."

Jane shuddered. "I am."

Mr. Cox stood and crossed the floor. "With all due respect, my lady. I must disagree." He placed his palm on her shoulder. "You were defending yourself."

"If only the Whitehaven sheriff could see it that way." She faced him, biting her lip. "I might gain a pardon."

Mr. Cox removed his cloak from the peg by the door. "That would be ideal, but until then you must remain here." He fastened the clasp at his neck and picked up the bulky parcel from the floor. "This wool is first quality. It will bring good coin and soon your larder will again be full."

From the sound of the splashing outside, the rain hadn't eased. "Are you sure you will not stay a bit longer? I've plenty of pottage for us both—besides, 'tis still spitting rain."

"I'd best be heading back—wouldn't want anyone to become suspicious of my absence."

Jane's chest tightened as she moved to the door. Max rose from his mat beside the hearth and joined her, wagging his tail as if anxious at the prospect of venturing outside. "Stay, Max." Jane placed her hand on the latch and regarded Mr. Cox. "When will I see you again?"

"I shall return with your supplies in a fortnight or two."

She wanted to reach out and embrace him, tell this grey-haired old man how much he'd grown to mean to her, but it wouldn't be proper. Though if he hadn't spirited her away the night she'd stabbed Roderick, she would no doubt be dead. Jane did, however, place her hand on his forearm. "I cannot thank you enough for all you have done to help me."

His eyes rimmed red. "If only it could have been more, my lady."

Swallowing back the tightness in her throat, she opened the door and a gust of cold March air blew in with a sheet of rainwater. Mr. Cox clutched his cloak closed and strode outside. Jane reached for him, but he proceeded beyond her grasp.

"Close the door," he called over his shoulder.

Max sniffed the air and backed further inside. The little spaniel had no intention of trotting out into the squall. Jane shut the door and looked at the dog. "'Tis just the pair of us again."

The chamber had a chill to it now Mr. Cox had gone. The head valet at Buttermere Castle, he was allowed some liberty, though he had been right when he said he would be missed if he stayed away too long.

At least Jane had Max to keep her company. She would have gone mad by now but for the dog. She even allowed the spaniel to sleep on the bed with her. He might not be as large as some, but he was warm and provided comfort when she lay awake listening to the nightly sounds of the forest. Every rustle of leaves, whoosh of wind and crack of thunder—it all seemed so much louder at night—so much more frightening.

Chapter Two

Alexander pushed through the inn's heavy door, met with a soothing whoosh of warm air. Water streamed from his plaid and bubbled out his boots as he strode toward the bar.

Beady eyes shifted his way and the noisy banter of the patrons ebbed to a hum. Alex glanced sidewise. There wasn't another plaid in sight. All the men wore leather breeches and a mixture of grubby black doublets and moth-eaten mantles. From the filth, this inn could very well be a den of thieves.

Above the bar was emblazoned a red Tudor rose with a crown over it. *The royal badge of England. Blast me miserable luck.* He splayed his fingers over his sword's hilt, itching to grasp it, but one errant move and he might have a nasty brawl on his hands. A fight he'd relish, but presently cared not for the odds.

At the table to his left, someone shook a set of dice then let them roll with a clatter of wood on wood. Ahead, a bear of an innkeeper stood with his fists on his hips, sporting a disagreeable scowl beneath a thick black beard.

Alexander aimed to procure a room, order a meal and keep to himself. The last thing he needed was to mix with this unsavory lot. As he neared the bar, the banter behind him rose in volume and a relieved whistle slid through his lips.

The innkeeper raised his chin and narrowed his black eyes.

Alex had to stoop to rest his elbow on the bar—a common problem for a tall man. "A pint of ale."

The innkeeper stared as if contemplating his next move then he placed his hands on the bar and leaned forward. "I'll give you one, and then I expect you to be on your way."

"Oh?" Alexander reached into his sporran and slapped down two pennies. "I was hoping ye might have a room. The squall blew me *birlinn* off course, and I need a place to camp for the night."

Without a word, the man turned to the barrel behind the bar, pulled the spigot and filled a tankard. Behind, chairs scraped the floorboards, followed by the door creaking open and slamming shut. Alex stole a backward glance—good, he was surrounded by fewer Englishmen.

"What do they call this village?" Alex asked.

"St. Bees." The man plunked the pint in front of Alexander and snatched up the coins.

"Hmm." He rifled through his memory. "I do no' recall ever hearing of a saint named Bees."

"That's probably because you're a daft Highlander."

Alex had taken an instant disliking to the innkeeper when he stepped inside. As any Highland laird, he wore a sword at his hip, a dirk in his belt, daggers in his hose and up his sleeves. How he would have enjoyed palming a wee blade and flinging it into the bastard's neck. He hated bloody England. All she was good for were ships ripe for the plundering. Alex kept his eye on the black-bearded bear while he sipped his pint. Christ, it tasted worse than piss.

He skulled the ale and wiped his mouth with his wet sleeve. Mercy, he was bloody cold. "What about that room? 'Tis only for the night."

"None available. Not for the likes of you."

Alex glanced over his shoulder. About a dozen patrons sat around tables, all looking as poor as beggars. He doubted a one had paid for a bed. "Ye have something against Scots?"

"Bloody oath I do."

Alex rolled his eyes to the cobweb-encrusted rafters. He didn't need a fight, but now he'd had a drink he was shivering to his boots. Next, his teeth would start chattering. The thought of weathering the night under a tarpaulin in the *birlinn* was none too appealing. *Perhaps if I tried a different tact.* "I can pay two crowns. That's twice what ye'd get from yer own countrymen."

"I said I've got no rooms, you bloody sheep-stealer," the innkeeper bellowed. "Now be off with you."

Alexander pushed away from the bar. The banter in the room stopped. When he turned, all eyes watched. *Miserable English hospitality.* His footsteps sloshed over the floorboards as he headed to the door. When he grasped the latch, a gale whipped it open and practically blew the thing from its hinges.

Normally Alexander would have clutched his cloak closed at the neck, but that luxury remained behind on the Isle of Raasay. He'd sailed off in such a hurry. All he had were the *birlinn*, the clothes he was wearing, his weapons and a sporran heavy with coin. At the time, he'd thought it plenty to take him away.

Away? Where in God's name is that?

Rain pelted from the sky while he walked through the muddy lane. Aside from the inn and a few cottages, St. Bees wasn't much of a village. Alex peered down the main road—didn't even see a church. *What kind of wretched lost souls live here?*

He didn't aim to find out. He always stowed a few things in the *birlinn*—a canvas tarpaulin and a handful of bully beef. That'd see him through until morning if the wind didn't blow him back out to sea.

A clap slapped water behind him.

Alexander's hackles stood on end. The wind and rain made a racket, but the sound wasn't droplets hitting puddles, nor was it from the rush of the wind.

It came again.

Then a hiss. He'd heard that sound hundreds of times, and it made his blood run cold.

Every muscle in his body tensed.

Steeling himself for a fight, Alex sped his pace and slipped his fingers around the hilt of his sword. His gaze darted over his right shoulder, then left. He counted only two. Heart thundering in his chest, he bellowed and whipped around, swinging his blade in an upward strike.

The two bastards crouched and trained their blades in a deadly challenge. The tallest one emitted a nervous laugh. "Give us your purse and we'll merely take your boat and be on our way."

"What if I say no?" Alexander lunged.

The man deflected the blow. The other attacked from the side. Whipping his blade in an arc, Alex defended. Using his sword's momentum, he advanced, driving his blade toward the thief's flank. The man skittered aside, but not far enough. Alex's strike sliced open his leg.

The brigand backed away. "The giant Scot's trying to murder me!"

The tall one cackled a hideous laugh and swung his blade in a circle. "The only beggar who'll be murdered this night is this flea-bitten sheep reiver." With a quick jab, the man advanced. Alex defended the blow in a battle of swords.

Just when he'd gained the upper hand, footsteps slapped the mud. Out of the corner of his eye, the bastards from the tavern approached. Alexander delivered the killing blow, planted his legs firm and prepared to face them. Armed with swords and battleaxes, a dozen men barreled toward him bellowing like skewered bulls.

A trained knight, Alexander fought with verve, but the blackguards wouldn't stop coming. Just when he'd cut one down, two more replaced him. His muscles burned as he fought, slowly backing toward the *birlinn*. But Alex was no fool. He'd be lucky to make it that far.

The pole from an axe crashed into his side with a jarring thud. A fist slammed into his mouth, another, his gut. The wind whooshed from his lungs with a grunt. Alex spun—right into the blunt end of a swinging poleaxe.

The world reeled. He tried to maintain his stance, but he could no longer discern up from down. His body crumpled to the ground. Out of control, the back of Alexander's head hit a rock. Before he could move, blackness shuttered his mind.

***

Alexander clapped a hand over his mouth and choked back a heave. The relentless pounding in his head was unbearable. The hard floor beneath him jostled and creaked. Horse hooves clomped upon a wet road.

Alex opened his eyes to be splattered by raindrops. He swiped a hand across his face. *Jesus, that hurt.* He touched his lip. That stung too. He tried to sit up, but a sharp jab in his ribs made him grunt.

"We can use a new fishing boat. This might be a good year for us after all," a deep voice said.

A reedy voice cackled. "What are you going to do with your share of the coin?"

"Don't know about you, but I'm heading to Whitehaven to find me a wench."

"Always thinking with your cock, are you not?"

The cart turned and the hoof beats muffled as if they'd moved from a stony road onto a path. Above, a covering of trees quelled the rain, though sloppy drops plopped around Alex.

"I hate this forest—it's been haunted ever since the monks were burned by the king's men," the deep voice said.

"We'd best dump the body afore the ghosts get after us."

"Just a bit further. Don't want the stench of rotting flesh to foul St. Bees. He's a bull of a man—he'll stink to high heaven."

Alexander tensed and felt for his sporran. Of course it was gone, as was his *birlinn*, and this miserable pair thought him dead. He reached inside his sleeves for his daggers. *Blast. They're gone, too.*

He'd have to fight the thieves with his fists. The cart hit a bump and jostled his body. His head throbbed so excruciatingly, stars crossed his vision. Again he tried to sit up, but dreaded blackness overcame his mind...

When Alexander next woke, the men had hold of his arms and legs.

"Jesus, the bastard's heavy," a straining voice said.

The fingers gripping his ankles dug in like a tourniquet. "Dump him in in the brush and let's be off."

"This place makes the hair on my arms stand on end."

His body swung and crashed onto the mossy forest floor with a thud. A stick protruded into his side. Alex grunted and opened his eyes. The miserable louts had dumped him without a second look. They hastened back to their cart, leaving him suffering and exposed to the elements.

Alexander could no sooner stand and fight than if he were dead—perhaps he was even closer to death.

It mattered not. He'd receive no sympathy from a pair of murderous thieves. He curled into a ball and cradled his pounding head between his hands while inhaling shallow pants to allay the pain breathing caused. Heaven help him, he mightn't survive the night.

Chapter Three

Jane finished the evening chores and sat in her rocker, emitting an enormous sigh. She held her hands up to the candlelight. At one time, she'd been proud of her smooth skin and her nicely manicured fingernails. But now, a different sense of pride filled her. The jagged nails and rough, callused palms were a testament to her new life. Never had she considered she would be living alone deep in a forest, but the solace it brought and the freedom from battering empowered her.

Yes, she had taken her husband's life and would probably be sent to the bowels of hell on Judgment Day, but given the choice, she would do it again. Eight years she'd survived under the tyranny of the Earl of Whitehaven. He'd beaten her until she could take no more.

Jane didn't even mind the water dripping from the soggy rafters above.

Max stirred on his rag rug in front of the hearth. The spaniel's ears pricked. Her heartbeat quickening, Jane held her breath and listened. The wind still blew with such force, the trees popped and rustled. A noise boomed. Jane jumped in her seat.

Max turned his head and growled.

Jane listened again, but her thundering heartbeat consumed her ears.

"Stop, Max. You're making me as nervous as a finch."

The dog hopped to his feet and barked—not a yip, but a ferocious, rumbling, growling roar.

Jane's heart nearly hammered out of her chest. She stood and spun full circle. Snatching the poker from the nail on the hearth, she then held it up like a sword, hands trembling out of control.

Max barked.

"Hush! I cannot hear a thing with your racket."

Slowly, she tiptoed toward the door with Max growling at her heels. Her breath rushing in her ears, Jane tried to listen for any unusual sound.

Max whimpered.

She glanced down. "What is it, boy?"

With a resounding bang, the door burst open. A crazed man gaped at her with piercing and anguished blue eyes. Grunting, he staggered inside and collapsed face first to the floor.

Max launched into a cacophony of barking, racing around the man as if the spaniel had made a conquest.

A cold wind chilled the cottage while Jane tried to steady the poker with both hands and point it at the burly form. He didn't move.

Max whimpered and licked the man's face. Then the dog curled up beside him.

Jane gaped. "Merciful father."

The wind continued to whip in through the doorway, blowing in leaves and spitting rain. Jane steeled her nerves, skirted around the beast and slammed the door. Standing with her back against it, she regarded the man leaking water onto her floorboards. He wasn't dressed like a local. He wore a plaid and a black leather doublet, hose to his knees with muddy boots. She tapped the sole of one with the poker.

He remained flaccid, all except for his calf muscle. It bulged and relaxed. She tapped again and his muscle bulged as large as a pumpkin. Afraid to try to touch him once more, she pressed her back to the door and cleared her throat. "I beg your pardon, but you cannot possibly stay on the floor…or anywhere nearby for that matter." She clutched the poker to her chest, terrified he might jump up and wallop her like Roderick would have done.

But the man, the Highlander, remained quite unconscious.

She'd heard stories about plaid-wearing barbarians from the north of Scotland. They were the most feared savages in all of Christendom. But that wasn't her first concern.

Whatever am I to do? If he recognizes me, I'll be burned at the stake by morning. She turned to the door and squeezed the latch. Peering outside, she saw no horse. *How did he come to be here?*

She closed it and regarded the Scot over her shoulder. He had a strong back and thick auburn tresses strewn across his face. He wore no sword belt, not even a dagger in his stockings. Jane tiptoed to his head. Stooping down, she brushed the hair away from his face and gasped. It was a handsome face, yet weathered and ruddy with lines etched deep at his eyes as if he spent a great deal of time working in the sun. Blood smeared across his temple and he had a split lip. She'd suffered such injuries in the past.

Jane smoothed his hair from his forehead and her fingers connected with a raised knot. *He's been beaten. Badly.* She held her breath and listened for a moment. If he was traveling with companions, they'd be nearby for certain.

She clasped praying hands to her lips. *Heaven forgive me, he cannot stay.*

Placing a hand on his shoulder, she shook him. "Excuse me, sir. Can you hear me?"

The Highlander did not respond, though his breathing became shallower.

Perhaps if he remains here until he wakes I can then send him on his way. After all, I cannot very well tie him to an ox and drag the poor soul back into Abbey Wood. Besides, I cannot in good conscience leave him to the elements in his condition. She emitted a long sigh. *I, myself, know what it is like to weather a blow to the head with a fist or worse.*

With resolve, Jane strode to her bedchamber. She retrieved a blanket and a pillow. After she'd stuffed the pillow under the Highlander's head and draped a blanket over his body, she turned the rocker to face him and sat.

With her poker in hand, she watched the sturdy male form. *When he wakes, I'll send him on his way, and that will be the end of it. Surely he will not try anything untoward, since I am armed and he obviously is not.*

***

Alexander opened his eyes. A dog licked him, leaving slobber across his lips. Grunting, Alex pushed the mutt away. The scruffy, liver-colored dog was too small to be of use to anyone. Alex rolled to his back and grunted again. Ballocks, everything hurt. His head throbbed and a sharp pain jabbed his ribs every time he took a breath. He licked his bottom lip. That stung too.

A creak came from his right. Alex raised his head slightly to find a woman sound asleep in a rocking chair. She clung to a fire poker resting across her lap. Her mouth slightly parted, she had high color in her cheeks and her linen coif sat askew atop her head, giving him an eyeful of flowing tawny tresses.

He glanced down at his disheveled plaid, doublet and shirt. *I must have given her an awful fright.*

Around him, water dripped from the rafters, collected by a half-dozen pots or so. *My oath, she'll nay have a cottage if the roof is no' repaired soon.*

He rested his head upon the pillow and closed his eyes. Heaven help him, he'd hit bottom. Not only had he lost his sea *birlinn*, he'd lost his weapons and his coin—definitely not a good position for a laird to be in when alone on foreign soil. Worse, his body was so stiff from injuries, he wouldn't be able to defend himself against the mangy mutt now curled beside his hip, let alone a human being.

He needed to heal and find a way back to Raasay to face his horrid past. Perhaps he could hire on as a hand and work on a transport until he reached home. The pain in his ribs jabbed like someone skewered him with a dagger. Alexander ground his molars. *What the blazes have I done?*

"You're awake?"

The woman's shrill voice made his eyes fly open. She jumped to her feet, brandishing the poker like she was about to beat him with the blasted thing. "Who are you?"

Alex grimaced as he pushed himself up and stood on wobbly pegs. He held his palms high. "Forgive me intrusion, madam. I am Alexander…ah…from the Highlands." He couldn't reveal his identity. If anyone discovered he was the Chieftain of Raasay, they might very well hold him for ransom.

She raised the trembling poker higher. "Have you no family name?"

"Nay—'tis oft the way in the Highlands," he hedged. "And what are ye called?"

She scooted back. "La…ah…Mrs. Howard." She seemed none too sure about it, but Alexander cared not. It was best if they kept things unfamiliar. Her damned poker shook at his nose. "How…how did you come here?"

Bloody oath, she had penetrating acorn eyes. He swiped his hand across his pounding head. He had not just allowed his miserable self to admire the woman's bonny eyes. He had no business admiring any woman ever again. "I had a wee skirmish by the St. Bees Inn. It seems the local folk do no' take kindly to Scotsmen."

"You have not been in these parts long, then?" Her clipped accent was high English, he was certain of it—all the more reason for the quandary—a bonny highborn woman alone in the wood, in the northwest of England?

"Nay, me wee *birlinn* was blown onto the beach by a nasty tempest. I tried to let a room at the inn, but none were to be had." He tenderly licked his split lip. "Then a mob of murdering bastards attacked, thieved me boat and coin and dumped me in the wood for dead."

She studied him as if trying to decide whether to bludgeon him or not, all the while the poker shuddering in her hands. But, Jesus, she looked too thin. Alexander again held up his palms to prove he was no threat, his legs still wobbly beneath him. "Ye have anything to eat?"

She shook her head along with her ridiculous poker. "Oh no, you cannot stay. You must leave straight away." Her voice warbled like a skittish bird.

He glanced around the shabby cottage. "From the looks of things, ye could use a hand." *I've got no other place to lick me wounds.*

"Absolutely not." She pointed the poker at the door. "Please, go."

Alex gave her a sidewise glance and scooted toward the hearth. A kettle hung over the embers. "Could ye offer a poor beggar a mere bowl of oats? Even the most miserly landowner wouldna turn a man away without a morsel of food."

That must have hit a chord with Mrs. Howard, because her eyes trailed to the cast iron pot too. "I've some pottage. But you must promise to leave immediately after you've broken your fast." Then her gaze shifted to a crest above the mantel.

Seems an odd place for such an extravagant coat of arms. But that, too, was none of Alexander's concern.

"My thanks." Stiff and aching, Alex grunted while he moved to the table with the dog on his heels. There wasn't a spot on his body that didn't hurt, and spending the night unconscious on the hardwood floor only added to his pain. He sat on a rickety bench. Good God, was everything in this cottage in need of repair? "From the looks of yer roof I'd reckon ye could use a strong back." *Where in devil's name is her husband?*

Mrs. Howard set a bowl of gooey-looking mush in front of him. "Spring's nearly upon us. I'll be able to make repairs once the weather turns."

"Aye?" He inhaled—the pottage smelled a wee bit better than it looked. "Do ye have someone to lend ye a hand?" He grimaced at a jabbing pain in his side.

She sat across from him, resting the poker in her lap. "Ah…of course." Lifting her spoon with a display of refined manners, she took a delicate bite. The dog jumped against her leg. "No, Max."

Alexander scooped a bite of pottage and nearly heaved. He glanced at the mutt and forced himself to swallow. "He's a puny lad. What breed is he?"

"A spaniel."

Och, the lass is full of information. "Ye dunna talk overmuch, do ye?"

"I daresay I am no longer used to talking." She clapped a hand over her mouth, her eyes wide as if she'd just revealed a treasured secret.

Alex shoveled in another bite. The second was more palatable—barely. "Ye wouldna have a spare sword or dagger ye could lend me?"

"Afraid not."

More clipped conversation, aye? Another sharp pang stabbed him in the ribs and made him jolt with a grunt.

"Are you in pain?"

Alex smirked. "I've been bludgeoned within an inch of me life, ye expecting me to jump up and dance a jig?"

"No." Snapping her eyes to her bowl, she stirred her mush. "Your breathing sounds shallow."

"'Tis because I've a busted a rib or two."

"Oh my heavens." She clapped a hand to her chest. "I am sorry."

I'm bloody sorry meself. "Ye wouldna have a roll of bandages to bind it with?"

Mrs. Howard's eyebrows drew together as if she were thinking. "I've a spare length of heavy holland cloth I use for a wimple."

He scooped his last spoon of pottage and forced it down. "I'd be grateful for a lend of it."

Her gaze met his for a moment. Something flickered deep inside his gut, a sensation he hadn't experienced since…since…God knew when. The look was followed by a sad smile, one that announced she'd been suppressing untold pain. Alexander resisted the urge to reach out and pat her arm, as he would do when consoling a soul from his clan. He must keep two things in the forefront of his mind—this was not Scotland, and he must conceal his true identity lest he put the whole of Clan MacLeod in peril.

The lass disappeared through a small doorway—the bedchamber, Alexander imagined. Alex glanced around the cottage, his gaze resting on the royal crest above the mantel. *Must represent the local noble family, I suppose.* Max rubbed against his leg and whined.

"Are ye hungry, mate?" The dog wagged its tail and spun in a circle. "Can I give Max a wee bit of yer pottage?" *'Tis most likely not fit for a dog either.*

Mrs. Howard stepped into view. "I'll do it." She crossed to the table and held out the heavy linen cloth. "With luck, this should wrap around your torso twice."

Standing, Alexander reached for it and his fingers lightly brushed hers. A subtle gasp escaped Mrs. Howard's lips. With a stare of alarm, she stepped back. Watching her eyes, the stirring in Alexander's gut churned faster. He quashed his unbelievably errant response by quickly clenching his muscles and bowing. "My thanks, m'lady."

She gave him a quizzical look, but didn't correct his use of *m'lady*. Then she gestured toward the door. "If you please, tell no one of our meeting."

"Very well." His head pounded when he straightened. He staggered forward, stumbling over a bucket near full with rainwater. Grasping the latch, he glanced over his shoulder. "Please pass along my gratitude to Mr. Howard."

"Go with God." She waved then bent down to hold the dog's collar. It didn't take a seer to realize Mr. Howard was long gone. But why the devil was this woman living alone with the place crumbling around her? That she couldn't cook worth a lick was clear. Alexander puzzled. What woman of noble birth could? Highborn women were bred for one thing—to birth sons to keep the nobility in power, just as it had been in his own family.

Once outside, he turned full circle. Where the hell should he go? *North? The next time I venture to St. Bees, I'll be heading there with a galleon sporting eighteen guns. Bloody oath, I'd blast the village off the map this day if I could.*

Mrs. Howard's cottage sat on a sizeable property surrounded by trees. Ahead was a path that looked more like a game trail—most likely it was the one he'd followed in the dark last eve. But the fence caught his eye. It was in such disrepair, he doubted the lady could keep any livestock at all.

Before he set out, he needed to wrap Mrs. Howard's wimple around his ribs. His every movement hurt with stabbing agony. He hobbled around back, finding things in the same poor condition.

No surprises, aye?

There was a coop with no door, and a flock of chickens foraged around the yard as if they owned the place. Yonder, a half-dozen shaggy sheep grazed in a paddock surrounded by a semblance of a fence. The wee beasties looked as if they'd missed their last shearing. Alexander spied the stable and wondered what disorder he'd find there, but at least it would give him privacy to examine his wounds.

Ahead, the apple orchard needed pruning, and fast. If Mrs. Howard didn't prune those trees, she'd see no fruit this season at all. But that was none of Alexander's concern. He'd made the second biggest mistake of his life sailing off in the *birlinn* without a crew.

He stepped inside the stable. Musty, he was surprised to see not a horse or heifer. A few chickens pecked at the moldy straw on the dirt floor. There were two empty stalls that looked in decent condition, but from the water streaks on the walls, the stable had a leaky roof just like the cottage.

Against one wall, iron tools were neatly hung—an axe, a scythe, a rake, shovel, shears, a two-man saw and an assortment of hand tools. A pair of stools sat pushed beneath an old workbench. *Odd, I expected to see everything scattered about the ground, gathering rust.*

Alexander removed his doublet and shirt and hung them on an empty peg. Just as he suspected, a black bruise the size of a cannonball spread across his ribs. He pressed against the swelling and hissed. No doubt, he was badly bruised at the least. But Alex was no stranger to pain. He needed to pull himself together and figure a way back to Scotland. *Aye?* He had a responsibility to return to Raasay...*eventually*. But to go back now grated almost as badly as the pain from drawing each breath. The memories were too raw.

Alex pressed the heels of his hands to his temples. If only his head would stop pounding.

When he grasped Mrs. Howard's cloth, the stable spun. He braced himself against the wall, but the spinning whipped around faster. His gut queasy as if he'd guzzled a jug of whisky. His legs wobbled. He dropped to his knees and doubled over, losing Mrs. Howard's tasteless pottage. Unable to move, Alex rolled to his side and closed his eyes. *I'll be up in a moment or two...*

$$Chapter\ Four$$

Jane clapped her hand to her chest and took a few deep breaths. The entire time Alexander was in the cottage, she'd feared for her life. The man was so enormous compared to her, and he had the most intense blue eyes she'd ever seen. They were almost predatory. Every time he looked at her, she trembled down to her toes. Thank the good Lord he didn't try to overtake her. Heaven only knows what would have happened if she'd been forced to wallop him with the poker.

She sat on the bench and chewed her nail—something her mother would have abhorred. She didn't like sending the Highlander away when he was obviously in pain, but his mere presence threatened her entire life. Jane also regretted lying to him about her name. However, as the daughter of the Earl of Nottingham, using her family name of Howard was not a complete lie—nor was the address *Mrs.*, she supposed.

Jane shuddered when her mind flashed to the night that had changed her life forever. Roderick had smelled of pickled brandy and was in one of his foulest moods. He'd chased her around the chamber with a candlestick. When he struck her in the back, she'd fallen to her knees. She remembered shielding her head from another blow and seeing the dagger sheathed and fastened to his belt. If she didn't stop him, he would have killed her. She knew it in the depths of her soul. Without thinking of the consequences, she snatched his knife from its scabbard. In one motion she'd sliced it across his throat.

Jane hadn't meant to cut him, only to wave the dagger in his face so Roderick would stop hitting her.

The blood had drained from his face so quickly.

In the last moments of Roderick's life, Jane crouched into a ball, frozen except for her trembling hands. If it hadn't been for Mr. Cox, she would have been taken into custody that very night. Doubtless, the Whitehaven sheriff would have tried her for murder and burned her at the stake.

The old valet had entered Roderick's chamber without a word. Then he'd quickly grasped her elbow and led her through the door that joined her chamber to the earl's. "...I'll gather some of your things into a satchel..." He'd managed it all while she stood stunned. "...You must go to my family's cottage in Abbey Wood. It has been standing empty for years..."

Jane had no recourse but to follow the man's every word, and for the past four months and nine days, Mr. Cox had shown her nothing but kindness, had given her a place to live and, moreover, a place to heal. After a time, he'd delivered a trunk with some of her gowns and personal effects. To help her survive, he'd slipped in a few head of sheep and chickens that wouldn't be missed from the vast Whitehaven flocks.

She'd taught herself to spin wool with the spinning wheel left in the bedchamber by Mr. Cox's mother, using wool she found stowed in a cupboard. Shearing the beasts this spring would prove a greater problem. Mr. Cox, at the ripe age of seventy, wouldn't be much help. She'd need to find a way to shear them, because there was no more wool left to spin. Yesterday Mr. Cox had taken her skeins of yarn, which would pay for her supplies in the near term.

Alas, when Alexander offered to lend a hand, she'd been so tempted to accept. But she could not.

Jane glanced up at the leaky roof, which had finally stopped dripping. True, the cottage needed a great many repairs, but it was her haven from the evil that lurked outside its walls. She'd grown comfortable here and the idea of anything threatening her home frightened her very core.

What if Alexander told someone he'd seen me? At least she hadn't given her true name, *and* he was a Scot. Surely he would try to stay clear of the locals as he made his way back to the border. The poor man. If only she could have done more to help him.

She sighed and stooped to scratch Max behind the ears. "At least the rain has ceased for a time. We can collect the eggs."

After feeding the dog the remaining pottage and emptying the pots filled with rainwater, she picked up her basket. "Come, Max." Every time the little dog scampered after her, she thanked her stars she'd found the stray—yet another lost soul who'd appeared on her doorstep only a fortnight after she'd arrived.

She pushed through the broken door of the chicken coop. That would soon be fixed, because she'd asked Mr. Cox to purchase a handful of nails. She wasn't trained in building or cooking or wood chopping, but she'd learned a great deal fending for herself. She reached into the nesting boxes. "Five eggs today, Maxie boy."

The dog yelped and spun in a circle. Why, Jane honestly believed the dog preferred eggs to her pottage. However, the stew might taste better if she got up the nerve to kill a chicken to add to it. On occasion, Mr. Cox would snap their necks and he'd shown her how to pluck and clean them. She'd even been saving the feathers to make pillows.

Jane stopped at the fence and watched the sheep graze. With winter over, grass was growing aplenty, and they were looking fat—or was it their ample puffs of wool? "Max, you shall have to help me muster them into the yard for shearing." She looked to the broken mess of wooden posts and rails Mr. Cox's father had once used as a holding pen to assemble the sheep before they were led into the stable to be shorn. It appeared more like a heap of wood ready for a bonfire.

Her shoulders slumped. She must figure out how to mend fences soon, else the sheep would scatter. Surrounded by a rock wall, the paddock they were in now was the only bit of land on the property that had somewhat secure fencing, but even it showed signs of disrepair.

She glanced into her basket of eggs—sustaining food she had collected herself. That made her stand a bit taller. "Max, we must go inside at once and make a list of all that needs to be done. We shall accomplish one thing at a time, and I'd wager by summer's end we'll…" She turned a full circle, but the little dog was nowhere in sight. "Max?"

To where on earth did he wander? Jane headed toward the orchard, when a whimper came from the stable. "Max?"

She stepped inside the dim room. Ahead, the dog yelped. Blinking to help her eyes adjust to the darkness, Jane gasped. Alexander lay with his back to her, unconscious on the stable floor, and Max was licking the poor man's face. Moreover, the Highlander had removed his shirt. His sculpted back muscles were more prominent than anything she'd ever seen, his skin riddled with white scars, as if he were no stranger to battle.

Jane hissed at the sight of the black bruise that spread along the side of his ribcage. "Oh my. His injuries are far worse than I'd imagined."

She knelt and brushed the dog aside. "Alexander, sir." She held out her hand and opened then closed her fist. She wanted to touch him, but it would be ever so improper. Steeling her resolve, Jane placed her palm on his warm shoulder and shook. "Please wake."

He lay completely still. Jane held a finger under his nose. Thank heavens a faint breath caressed it. She covered her mouth. At least he no longer posed a threat inside the cottage. But what on earth should she do with him? He'd complained of a headache as well as sore ribs. Perhaps he should drink some willow bark tea when he woke—she knew how to prepare that.

"Max, stay."

Jane dashed to the cottage, grabbing some wood along the way. After she'd stoked the fire, she hung the kettle to boil some water. Then she set to mixing a batch of kettle scones—Mr. Cox had shown her how. He said they were easier than making bread.

Now what? As soon as he wakes, feed him and hope he's well enough to be on his way by morning? She opened the shutter and peered through the wood. *What if someone comes looking for him?*

She added lard to the flour, a pinch of salt, leavening and some water. Stirring furiously, she imagined a whole army of brawny Highlanders descending upon Abbey Wood and surrounding her tiny cottage.

Jane spooned a dollop of dough into the big cast iron kettle. *Stop it, Jane. He said himself he was dumped and left for dead.* She scooped another dollop and swiped an errant strand of hair away from her face. *But what if his kin are looking for him? He said nothing about traveling companions or his home aside from the Highlands.*

Her stomach roiled. *Clansmen from the wild Highlands could be searching for him this very minute.*

Straining with effort, she lifted the kettle and hung it on the articulating arm. Henceforth, Lady Jane would have a far greater appreciation for all the work servants did.

She clapped the flour from her hands and faced the door. "As soon as he rouses, I must uncover more about him—ensure no more unexpected guests happen upon my doorstep."

***

Alexander awoke to the call of birds. Again his head rested upon a pillow and a blanket covered him, but this time, the ground beneath was far softer than it had been in the cottage. He rubbed his eyes and sat up. Beside him rested a tankard containing liquid and a wooden plate with some pasty-looking scones.

Alas, he recalled collapsing in the stable. He peered through the doorway. Mist shrouded his view, but he could tell daylight was anon. He must have been unconscious a whole day.

Ever so thirsty, he picked up the tankard and guzzled greedily. Sticking his tongue out, he spat. "Christ, what sort of chalky, bitter brew is this?" Dubiously, he reached for the scone. If he weren't half starved, he'd give the food a pass. Nothing Mrs. Howard had prepared was fit for consumption. No wonder the woman was so thin. Alex doubted she'd be able to eat her own cooking. But when he bit into the pastry, his mouth watered. "Mm." *Perhaps Mrs. Howard should live off her scones.*

He washed it down with another gulp of her bitter brew and something clicked. He'd drunk this before. It was willow bark tea, given to him by Friar Pat on Raasay. He regarded the tankard and smiled. Mayhap Mrs. Howard was concerned for his health.

Standing, he stretched to test his bruised ribs—not quite as sore as yesterday, but it still hurt to take a deep breath. Perhaps spending a day unconscious had helped him heal. The pounding in his head had ebbed a bit too.

After he polished off the second scone, he regarded the tools on the wall. *I could help the lass afore I set out. After all, it would be obvious to a blind man she needs a charitable soul.*

He pulled the shears from the wall, grabbed a rickety old ladder and lumbered to the orchard. Of all the things he'd noticed yesterday, pruning was the direst chore in his mind. Mrs. Howard needed food. She could not only eat apples, she could make cider and tarts. Alexander licked his lips. *A tart would go down nicely 'bout now.*

Reaching up to trim the high branches hurt so badly, it made his eyes water, but after the first half-dozen trees, his body grew somewhat impervious to it.

Max bounded from the cottage, racing toward Alexander with a ferocious bark. The dog jumped up against the ladder. It teetered and Alex latched on to a branch. The blasted thing cracked and snapped.

"Argh!" Alexander tried to swing his feet beneath him to break his fall, but he crumpled to the ground in a heap. Lying on his back, the sharp pain in his ribs punished him with an extra bit of throbbing.

Max licked his face.

"Ye bloody mongrel dog."

"Oh my heavens." Mrs. Howard came running. "Are you hurt?"

Alexander swallowed back his agony. "Just a few more bruises to add to the ones that were already there."

"Bad dog." She shook her finger, and Max circled around her with his ears back and tail between his legs.

Alexander grunted as he stood. "Och, the dog was just excited to see me."

"I daresay he slept beside you all afternoon until I made him come in for the night."

"Aye?" Alex bent to straighten the ladder, swallowing his urge to bellow with the jarring pain.

Mrs. Howard planted her fists on her hips. "And whatever are you doing out here after being unconscious?"

"I thought I'd lend ye a hand afore I took me leave." He picked up the shears. "If these trees are no' pruned in the next sennight, ye'll see no harvest at all."

"Oh?" She smoothed her fingers over her chin. "Mr. Cox didn't tell me that."

Another piece of the mystery unfolds. "And who is he?"

"Ah…" She blushed redder than the apples these trees would bear. "He's the man who let me the cottage."

Alex repositioned the ladder and climbed. "Well, 'tis good to ken ye're no' out here in the wood without a soul to check on ye."

"And what of your family? Are they not missing you?"

He snipped a branch. The last thing he wanted to do was talk about his kin. Yet the tickle at the back of his neck told him they would be looking. His brother Ian wouldn't want to step in as laird for long. And then there was his son, Malcom. Only two years of age, Alexander's mother, Lady Anne, would tend to the bairn's needs until he returned to Raasay. But he didn't want to think about any of it right now. He glanced down at Mrs. Howard. She crossed her arms, waiting for an answer. "Alas, m'lady, I have no family."

Though the lie bit, he couldn't bring himself to tell the truth.

Her face brightened a smidgen. "No one will be out looking for you, then?"

"Not that I'm aware of." The second lie was easier. "I'll prune yer trees and be on me way."

She bowed her head. "Well then, I thank you, and there will be an extra ration of kettle scones for your abounding kindness. Come, Max." She started back toward the cottage, but stopped. "Have you ever killed a chicken before?"

He'd killed for food, killed in battle… "Aye, m'lady."

With a sharp gasp, she clapped her hand to her chest. "Would you mind killing a chicken before you take your leave? I haven't quite the stomach for it."

He gave her a lopsided grin. "Any bird in particular?"

"No. Mayhap a plump hen."

"I shall have it to ye by midday so ye can prepare the chicken for yer supper, m'lady." He watched her reaction again. Referring to her as "m'lady" most definitely disturbed *Lady* Howard.

Chapter Five

Jane spent the morning foraging for vegetables to add to a new pottage. The last one she'd made contained only barley and leek with no meat at all. The thought of adding fresh chicken made her stomach rumble. She'd dropped quite a bit of weight fending for herself. At Buttermere Castle, she could clap her hands and servants would appear with anything she fancied, as long as it was in season. Oh how spoilt she'd been. Now she'd eat her wimple if forced. *Please, may things never become that bad.*

True to his word, Alexander knocked on the door—of course he was the only person she could imagine doing so. When she opened it, he held out a featherless chicken, his white teeth almost sparkling beneath his growth of coppery beard. "Killed, plucked and gutted, for yer supper as promised."

She took the naked bird. "My thanks, but what have you done with the feathers?"

"They're back by the wood stack where I butchered the hen. If ye'd like, I could fetch them."

"That would be ever so kind. I'm saving the downs to make pillows."

"I should have thought as much. May I have a lend of yer basket?"

After she'd handed it to him, Alexander was not gone but a moment when another rap resounded at the door. Jane's heart fluttered. A completely inappropriate reaction. She clapped her hands to her cheeks and took a deep breath. *He's well enough to be on his way now.*

She opened the door and he grinned, his dark eyes not only friendly, but deep, unspoken emotion lurked behind them. Sadness, perhaps? She took the basket. "Thank you. Were you able to prune all the trees?"

"Aye, at least what I could reach." He clasped an arm around his ribs as if they were causing pain. "I didna thank ye for leaving the willow tea and scones."

"'Twas the least I could do." She crossed to the board and wrapped the last of the kettle scones in a cloth. "Here, take these. I wish I had coin to pay for your kindness."

He opened the cloth and shoved a whole scone in his mouth. "My thanks. A man works up an appetite with a bit o' labor."

Oh heavens, if only I had more food to give him. "So, you'll be heading back to Scotland, then?"

"I'll no' be heading to St. Bees, that's for certain." He shrugged. "Is there anything else I can do for ye, m'lady?"

Jane bristled every time he addressed her as his lady. How did he know she was nobly born? She was wearing a plain kirtle and a peasant's wimple. "I daresay you've done more than enough. I am ever so grateful for your kindness." She bowed her head. "Go with God."

***

Outside, Alexander stared at the door while it closed. He'd harbored a modicum of hope that Mrs. Howard would invite him in. Truth be told, his ribs still hurt like hell, especially after he'd fallen off the ladder. Sure, working had helped take his mind off the pain, but setting off through the English countryside injured, without a weapon, wearing a plaid, was a surefire way to end up dead.

He stuffed the remaining scone in his mouth. He could use a bit of that chicken Mrs. Howard was fixing to crucify with her cooking. He wondered if she had a spit by her hearth. The bird would be all the more tasty if it were roasted rather than boiled.

He started toward the path when Max yipped and ran in beside him. *Christ.* "Ye cannot go with me." He held his palm to the dog's nose. "Stay."

The dog sat and cocked his head to the side with questioning ears.

"I mean it. Stay."

Proceeding on, Alex took note of fallen trees aplenty, and rushes that could be used to repair the roof. Mrs. Howard had everything she needed to set the farm to rights—if she knew how. If her ability at the hearth was any indication, his guess she'd been bred into nobility was spot on.

Alex made it about a mile into the forest when Max bounded after him. "I told ye to stay." Hellfire, the thing was cute, wagging his tail. But Mrs. Howard needed the dog far more than Alex did. He pointed. "Go back."

The blasted mutt spun in a circle and jumped on Alexander's leg with a look that threaded itself around his heart. "Hop down. Now off with ye."

But Max would have none of it.

"Och damn-it-all, I'll take ye back, but ye mustn't follow me again. Mrs. Howard is going to think me a right royal pest."

Ever so happy with himself, Max danced in front of the door while Alexander swallowed his pride. This was the third time he'd knocked on the lady's door this day, and she'd already sent him on his way—made it clear she didn't want him around. But he reached up with his fist and rapped.

Footsteps pattered inside. "Who is it?" Her voice had a tremor.

"Alexander again, m'lady. Apologies, but a certain pet of the four-legged variety saw fit to follow me."

The door whipped open. Mrs. Howard had red splotches on her face and she dabbed her nose. Had she been crying? Alexander resisted the urge to step inside and pull her into a consoling embrace. Doing so was not only improper, but it would undeniably confound the lady. She'd most likely slap him across his split lip.

She turned her attention to the dog. "Max, you mustn't wander off." She swiped both hands down her face. "I am sorry you had to turn back."

He batted his hand through the air. "'Tis nothing."

They stood there awkwardly for a moment. Alexander bit the inside of his cheek, wishing she'd invite him inside to share her meal of chicken—no matter how she'd ruined it. He hadn't had a bite of meat in days. A few scones weren't enough to sustain a warrior, even one who'd spent the day pruning apple trees.

She started to close the door. "Well, I must thank you yet again."

He held his arm straight out and stopped the door's momentum. "Look here, m'lady. I've no place to go and I'm in no condition to defend meself."

She dropped her jaw as if to object, but Alex continued. "I ken ye've some dark secret ye do no' want me to hear, but as clear as the nose on me face, ye need help."

"But—"

"I'll hunt and provide ye with meat. I'll mend yer fences and yer roof and then I'll be on me way with nary a question asked."

Eyes wide, she bit her bottom lip—a sign she liked his idea.

Alexander stood firm. "I'll not take no for an answer."

She released her grasp on the door. "You cannot sleep in the cottage."

"Aye, I'll set up a pallet in the stable."

"You...you'd best take your meals out there as well."

Alex gaped. Lord, she drove a hard bargain. A lot of work for a wee bit of food and the prospect of enjoying it with the sheep shite out the back. "Och. Aye, I'll eat in the stable with Max if that's what makes ye happy."

"Very well." Her gaze darted to the trees, her lovely eyes narrowing as if she feared something grave beyond the forest. "But when the fencing and the roofing have been completed, you shall promise to go and never mention a word about your time here."

"Aye, m'lady. That's me plan as well."

***

Jane closed the door and wrung her hands. Had she just invited the Highlander to stay? Yes, but he'd said himself he didn't care about her secrets, and he knew no one from England, *and* he had no family looking for him. She looked at the pots and buckets scattered across the floor. She'd been praying for help, and now that it had arrived she worried about all the reasons she should send it away.

How much time would he need, both to heal and to make the repairs that required a strong back? A fortnight? Two? She shook her head. *An entire month is far too long. I'll give him a fortnight and then insist he go.*

The sun was setting when Jane carried a bowl of chicken pottage to the stable. "Hello?" Stepping inside, the floor had been raked clean, and smelled of cut rushes and something else, something distinctly male. It made the gooseflesh rise upon her skin.

Alexander stepped out from a stall. He'd tied his shoulder-length tresses away from his face. One strand of hair hung over his eye, making him look devilishly handsome. "Hello, m'lady. I was hoping I wouldna need to rap on yer door and bother ye again."

Her insides jumping like bacon in a fry pan, she turned away and set the bowl on the workbench. Evidently he planned to continue calling her "my lady," and she'd best not correct him, else it lead to more questions about her past. "I brought your supper."

"My thanks." He grinned, causing the fluttering to flit out of control, right up through her throat. Alexander gestured to the stall. "I made a pallet of rushes and a bit o' straw. It will be right comfortable."

She stepped beside him and peered through the dim light. He had the pillow and the blanket neatly placed, ready for sleep. "You need a candle out here to cast some light."

He smiled. Her insides fluttered. She must discourage his grinning.

"That would be a luxury I'd appreciate," he said.

When Jane turned, her shoulder brushed his chest. The image of his naked and scarred torso flashed through her mind, making her cheeks burn. He seemed not to notice, and pointed to the tools. "I aim to sharpen your scythe and axe. I saw a number of fallen trees in the forest that will suit for fence posts and rails."

"Indeed?" Jane had not been off the property since she'd arrived, and a good deal of that time, the ground had been wet or frozen. "Do you think you should give your ribs a chance to heal before you start in on the heavy labor?"

He shrugged. "A man works through the pain. Besides, the cloth ye lent me to bind them helps. The willow tea, too."

"Would you like some more? It wouldn't take me but a moment to brew it."

"Nay, no' now. I prefer something stronger with the evening meal."

Jane clapped a hand over her mouth. She hadn't thought to bring him something to drink. "I've watered wine in the cottage. Would you care for some?"

"My thanks, m'lady." He reached for the bowl and sniffed the pottage, followed by a cringe.

She bit her fingernail. "Oh dear, I'm afraid I'm not much of a cook, either."

"Yer scones are right delicious." He took a bite. "Mm. This is no' near as bad as the last batch."

Her cheeks now burning clear up to her ears, Jane excused herself and headed to retrieve the wine. *Merciful heavens, what country woman cannot cook? No wonder he calls me "my lady." He probably believes me the imposter I am.*

She pattered through the door. Mr. Cox brought a cask of watered wine every time he paid a visit, and fortunately it was far more than she could consume in a fortnight. She pulled the stopper and poured a tankard full for medicinal purposes—as long as he didn't fall into his cups. She hesitated. A drunken man could turn into a monster. She carefully poured a bit back into the cask and pushed in the cork.

Now to go out there, hand him the tankard and refrain from looking him in the eye. I cannot invite friendship of any sort, and those blasted blue eyes make swarms of butterflies flit around in my belly as if I were a young maid. Jane straightened her wimple, gathered a tallow candle and a flint, picked up the tankard and headed out. She wouldn't chat this time. She'd simply remain aloof like a proper Englishwoman and be on her way…with Max.

Alexander had finished the pottage when she stepped inside. He pointed to a rickety stool. "Would ye care to have a seat?"

She handed him the wine and set the candle on the board. "Mayhap for a moment." There she went, disobeying her own good sense.

Alexander used the smooth side of a rasp to strike the flint. "My thanks for the candle."

She sat a bit straighter. "I made it myself."

His eyebrows drew together. "I would assume so, m'lady."

Of course, Jane, you dolt. Country women make their own everything. She glanced to the candle, ever so happy the wick was burning as if she'd been making tallow candles all her life. Pushing aside her own advice to head back to the cottage, she gave in to her curiosity to discover more about him and most definitely steer the conversation away from her. "You never told me why you were sailing though the Irish Sea."

A shadow passed over his face, as if he harbored a secret as horrible as hers. He pulled the other stool from under the workbench and sat across from her. "After I buried me wife, I couldna stay, so I tied a rope to the rudder of me *birlinn* and sailed down the coast."

"You lost your wife?" She tapped her palm to her chest. "I am so sorry."

"She was a good woman…" His voice trailed off as if he didn't care to talk about it.

Jane understood his reluctance all too well and opted to change the subject. "Isn't it dangerous to sail a sea vessel alone?"

"Aye, 'tis meant to be manned by six, but I was daft enough to think I could manage on me own."

Jane tensed. "So you *do* have a clan? People who will be looking for you?" Heaven help her, she should not have invited him to stay.

He held up his palm and gave her the most reassuring smile she'd ever seen come from a man. "Ah, m'lady, ye are an intelligent lass, but I doubt me clan will be sending out a search party. They ken I'll be back when I'm ready."

"Did you tell them as much?"

"More or less." He looked at her with those deep blue eyes—
eyes that appeared to be filled with a lifetime of suffering.

The urge to reach out and offer a reassuring touch came over
her. But Jane clasped her hands together and squeezed. Beyond the
doorway, the day's light had faded.

She should go.

Alexander's skin flickered with amber in the candle light. She'd
never seen a man so ruggedly handsome. And the way he looked at
her stirred a yearning deep inside, similar to the feeling she'd had
when she'd first started courting Roderick, but this deep yen ached far
stronger.

Alexander sipped his watered wine and smiled.

Jane took in a quick gasp. How long had she been sitting there
staring at him? She stood. "I'd best leave you to sleep."

Immediately he was on his feet, as a gentleman would be. "Must
you?"

He stepped so close, Jane swooned when she inhaled the spicy
musk she'd noticed when first entering the stable. Except this time,
the potency was intoxicating. She clapped a hand to her chest to quell
the sudden aching in her breasts. "W-with spring upon us, there is
much to do on the morrow."

He grasped her hand and rubbed it between his warm palms. Her
breath stuttered at his touch. Such a simple gesture, yet somehow it
carried unspoken tenderness. Mesmerized by the strength of his large
hands—hands that knew what it was like to carry out a day's honest
labor, Jane watched his fingers swirl. How long had it been since
she'd received a kindly touch from another?

Though rough and callused, he handled her with gentleness.
"Aye there is work aplenty, m'lady." His eyes twinkled before he
bowed, her palm still in his.

Jane stood dumbly while she watched him, as if she were the
downiest feather floating on a breeze. Alexander's warm breath
caressed her skin. Gooseflesh spread up her arm and tingled at the
back of her neck. Her heart hammered a rhythm so fierce, she could
scarcely breathe.

When his gentle lips caressed the back of her hand, Jane's own
lips parted as if her body craved for him to kiss her mouth. While he
straightened, she hoped he might. With long, coppery lashes, he
shuttered those soulful pools of blue and glanced at her lips. She
leaned toward him. Then his gaze flickered a tad lower before it
snapped to her face with his white-toothed grin.

"Goodnight, m'lady."

Chapter Six

A fortnight later, Alex rose early and headed to the paddock to resume fencing. Though his ribs still ached, breathing had become a bit easier. He'd learned as a lad that driving himself hard was the best cure for any ailment.

However, he still considered himself a wretched lout. Ever since he'd kissed Mrs. Howard's hand, he'd regretted it. Heaven help him, the English lady constantly consumed his thoughts. He needed to assuage his feral attraction to her, but by the saints, she stirred within him a deep-seated longing he'd never before experienced.

His marriage to Ilysa had been arranged when he was but ten and seven, and he'd scarcely met the lass before they were wed. Alexander had never found Ilysa attractive, though she wasn't overly displeasing. She simply was. They hadn't many interests in common, either. Mostly, they kept to their own chambers and presented an air of harmony when at clan gatherings. It seemed they were both content to live somewhat separate lives, rarely coupling. Though he'd grown to care for his wife and respect her as the mother of his bairn, he had never in his life behaved like a lovesick fool—a damned good thing, especially for a clan chieftain.

But every time Mrs. Howard came within ten feet, his male senses homed in upon her—could think of nothing else. His body craved her more than food. With the lady's every smile, he wanted to reach out and brush his fingers over her silken cheek, or grasp her hand and run kisses all the way up her arm until he claimed her mouth for himself.

Am I seeking solace from the pain, the guilt of losing Ilysa? Most likely.

When he'd shown Mrs. Howard how to tie the rushes for the roof repairs, it had taken every bit of self-restraint not to wrap her in his arms and crush her against his body. It was a good thing the perimeter fence repairs would be done soon, because he needed to be on his way...once the roof was repaired and the sheep were shorn.

A thwack sounded in the wood. Alex grinned. One of his snares had finally caught something.

The cottage door opened and Mrs. Howard stepped out. "What was that noise?" Her voice had a tremor like a skittish bird.

He pointed his thumb over his shoulder. "One of the traps, for certain."

Her face lit up with a radiant smile. "You caught something?"

Alexander rested the post against the fence. "I'd reckon so. I'll go check."

"Let me fetch my cloak and I'll join you. This I must see."

True to Alexander's word, a wee pig was snared by the hind leg.

Mrs. Howard clapped her hands. "A pork pottage will last a very long time indeed."

Oh no, he wasn't about to let her destroy this tasty bit of meat. "I beg yer pardon, but a sow this size ought to be roasted on a spit."

Her face brightened as if she thought Alex a genius. "Oh, that does sound delicious."

"Aye, and I'll be the one to tend it." Alex picked up a heavy branch. "Now turn your head, Mrs. Howard. A fine lady like ye shouldna have to see this."

She did as he requested. Bless it, the woman couldn't even kill a chicken. How she survived out here alone was beyond Alexander's reasoning. He made quick work of killing the wee beasty and slung it across his shoulders.

"What goes well with roast pork?" she asked.

"Do ye have any apples stowed from last season?"

"No...ah...I have no idea if Mr. Cox put them up or not." She shot Alexander a worried look and covered her mouth.

He let it pass, as he had many slips of her tongue. Alex figured Mrs. Howard hadn't been in the cottage all that long, else she would have better sense about things, like survival. "In Scotland the crofters dig out a wee hole beneath their cottages, put their winter stores in there and cover it over with stones to keep the vermin out."

"What a good idea."

"Of course if ye have room for a cellar that would be preferable." He almost mentioned the enormous larder kept cool by thick stone walls and dirt floor at Brochel Castle. They stored all manner of food year round, including meat. But admitting so would have revealed too much about his identity. Mrs. Howard was so skittish about the possibility that someone might be scouring the countryside looking for him, he'd been very careful about what he said. "Nonetheless, applesauce is delicious with roast pork."

"Mm. The idea makes my mouth water."

The day's fencing forgotten, Alexander formed a fire pit with stones and soon had a crackling flame. While the wood burned to coals, he pounded two Y-shaped branches either side and stripped the bark from a sturdy branch to turn the pork. Then he cleaned and skinned the beast and set it to roasting, planning to turn it every now and again until the end, when he'd spin the spit to ensure the pig was evenly cooked. Living on bland pottage and porridge for the past weeks, he could already taste it.

To further make use of the hot coals, Alex fetched the rusted iron arrow mold from the stable and an old kettle. He'd found a hunk of lead in the paddock—just the right size to fashion a dozen arrowheads or so. He put the kettle directly on the glowing coals and dropped in the lead. Max trotted up and sat beside him.

Alex glanced over his shoulder to see if Mrs. Howard had accompanied the dog, but she'd yet to make an appearance. "Ye ready for a feast, too, are ye, lad?"

Max spun in a circle and wagged his tail.

"Too right, laddie. We're all hankering for a good meal."

Alexander kept an eye on the lead whilst he turned the meat.

The cottage door clicked shut. He didn't need to turn to know Mrs. Howard approached. The slight tremor in his fingers, the tightness in his chest, the stirring of his manhood were the now familiar signs she was near.

She stepped beside him, bathing him in the scent of wildflowers and woman. "What have you got there?" She wore only a linen coif atop her head. Uncovered tresses flowed down her back in waves that resembled a field of wheat blown by a breeze. He liked it when he could see her thick, tawny locks. If only he could run his fingers through them.

But Alex scratched his wiry beard instead. Bloody oath, he needed a sharp knife to scrape off his whiskers. She probably thought him a barbarian. "Making some arrows to hunt with."

Mrs. Howard inspected the pot. "Is that lead?"

"Aye, found the piece over yonder." He turned the carcass. "Thought I could melt it down whilst I tended the spit."

"Excellent. Who knows, perhaps we'll have venison for our next meal."

"Have ye seen any deer about?"

"Not lately, but I've oft seen them grazing in the pasture."

Alex licked his lips. "All the more reason to have a few arrows on hand." He glanced at her. The sunlight sparkled in her hair and made it shimmer with gold. He couldn't resist. Reaching behind her, he caught a wisp in his palm and let it slide off. *Smoother than silk.* "Have ye ever used a bow?"

"Archery?" she asked, unaware he'd just touched her hair. "I was quite good at it when I was young."

He chuckled. "Ye're no' old now."

"Sometimes I feel much older than my years."

"If ye do no' mind my asking, what is yer age?"

She blushed. The woman would blush if you asked her how many eggs she'd collected that morn—certainly not the response of an old maid. "Eight and twenty."

"'Tis nothing." He thumped his chest. "I meself am *nine* and twenty."

Her breath caught and she gazed up at him. There it was, that connection that made every fiber of his body want to take her in his arms and carry her into the cottage bedchamber. If only he could have felt half as much desire for Ilysa. Alexander clenched his jaw, his fists, his bum cheeks to quell the longing. *God's teeth, I'm daft.*

She stared for a moment and then blinked in rapid succession. "Forgive me. You have been such a marvelous help, and I've not been an accommodating hostess."

"I—"

She held up per palm. "Please. I'd like you to dine in the cottage tonight. If you would bring in the pork when 'tis ready, I shall take care of the rest."

Radiant as the sun, Mrs. Howard was undeniably adorable when she put on her lady of the manor airs. Alexander bowed and tapped his forehead. "Until then, m'lady."

After he'd used up all the lead and turned the arrows into a bucket of water to cool them, Alex tested the pork and nearly dropped to his knees. Not only was it cooked to perfection, it tasted succulent and juicy. Max yipped and Alexander pulled off a morsel for the dog. "I'd better wash up if I'll be dining at the high table this eve." Alex chuckled. His place at Brochel Castle was at the center of the high table. Funny, he hadn't missed it these past weeks.

He cleaned up as best he could at the water barrel, pulled his hair back, tied it with a thong and headed into the cottage with the pork, hoping to God he'd be able to conceal the ridiculous lustful urges growing stronger by the day.

When she opened the door, Alexander nearly dropped the pig. Lustful urges be damned. Heaven help him, she was stunning. Wearing a red silk mantle over a richly embroidered kirtle of gold, Mrs. Howard topped the ensemble with a matching French hood trimmed with sable. He'd guessed before, but now he had absolutely no doubt the lady was of noble birth. He'd only seen gowns this lavish at court—aside from those his mother wore, but she was the daughter of an earl.

He must have been standing there for some time with his mouth gaping wide, staring at the creamy white mounds of succulent flesh peeking above her bodice. Mrs. Howard—if that was indeed her name—cleared her throat and stepped aside. "Will you not come in, Sir Alexander?"

How the bloody hell did she know he'd been knighted? He bowed and proceeded inside. "Ye look beautiful." He walked to the board and set the roast upon a large trencher. "But why don your finery for the likes of me?"

"Why not?" She closed the door. "I have a few things remaining from my former life, why should I not enjoy them this eve?"

When he turned, she was inches from him. God's teeth, she smelled like she'd bathed in a valley of rose petals. The image that conjured made him sway in place. He grasped her shoulders to avoid trampling her. She huffed and held her palms in front of her face as if she was afraid he might hit her. Quickly, Alex removed his hands and bowed his head. "Forgive me." What was he thinking, placing his hands on the lady?

"Of course." She nervously brushed her skirts and gestured to the table. "I found the apples and we shall have applesauce with our meal."

His stomach squeezed. *Must have been caused by the hunger.* "Ye are a wonder, m'lady."

"I most certainly am not, but I can follow instructions." She gestured to the meat. "I daresay you are the wonder, my lord."

Alex lost all joviality. "There is no need to call me your lord, m'lady."

"Oh? But you insist on calling me 'my lady.'" She pointed to a chair. "Shall we sit?"

After taking a seat, he picked up an eating knife. Succulent juice dribbled down the roast whilst he sliced a portion and set it on her pewter plate. She'd even brought out the fine tableware for this meal, with all the candles lit and the tankards filled with watered wine. If only she had told him this would be a fancy gathering, he would have spent a bit more time cleaning up. "Do ye have a razor or a sharp knife? I'm afraid me beard is taking over me face."

"I've a dagger you can use, but I rather like your rugged looks." Her smile turned seductive when she placed a wee piece of pork on her tongue, closed her eyes and sighed. "Mm. I do believe this is the best piece of meat I have ever eaten in my life."

His loins stirred to life with his chuckle. "That's because ye have no' had a decent meal in some time."

Her eyebrows arched. "I've been getting along nicely, thank you."

Alex dunked his meat in the applesauce and shoved a big bite in his mouth so he wouldn't need to reply. He, too, salivated at the taste.

After they were both fully satiated, he savored the fruity wine and watched her. The color in her cheeks was high this eve, as were her lips. Had she rouged them? Their gazes met. His mouth suddenly dry, Alexander's Adam's apple bobbed. He forced himself to look away—straight at the bedchamber door. *Damnation.*

"Do you like music?" Mrs. Howard asked.

He blinked. "Aye, very much, especially pipers."

"My favorite is the harp."

"'Tis a good choice. Do ye dance?"

She swayed as if a tune were playing. "Before I...ah...at one time, I could have danced all night."

He liked how she'd begun to open up to him. Alexander stood and bowed. "May I have this dance, m'lady?" He offered his hand.

"No." She clapped a hand to the white swells of breasts which peeked above her bodice. Frowning, Lady Howard sat upright. "I mustn't."

He grasped her delicate fingers and tugged. "Come." He hummed a few bars of a slow *almain.* She relented and allowed him to lead her to a clear space on the floor. He continued humming while the courtly steps came back to him.

Her eyes glistened. "You've been to court, sir knight."

"Aye, but ye tease me, m'lady."

She chuckled. "I think not." Mrs. Howard proved light on her feet while Alexander grasped her petite hands and twirled her in a circle. Step brush hop, step brush hop—it was as if they'd both learned from the same dance master.

Her skirts skimmed his calf. Licking his lips, he pulled her a tad closer to enjoy more of the silken damask titillating his legs. If only he could pull her into his arms and smother her ruby lips with a kiss.

The lady's mantle slipped from around her shoulders, revealing more of her low-cut neckline. Alex could not pull his gaze away from the milk-white skin and the perfectly formed breasts pushing against her stomacher.

They weren't dancing anymore. Had he done something wrong? Did she catch him staring at her incredibly delectable flesh? He met her gaze. Devil's bones, those almond-shaped eyes were made for sin. "Why did ye stop?"

"Your humming ceased." She brushed her fingers along his bearded cheek. "The deep bass of your voice moved me." Her words came out breathless.

Alexander stared into those divine acorn eyes, consumed by his desire to kiss her. Ever so slowly, he inclined his head. Her honeyed breath caressed his face and she closed her eyes. Their lips met with an explosion that sent his insides into a maelstrom of longing.

At long last, he gathered her into his arms and clutched her to his body, his senses filling with the delicious taste of woman. She didn't resist, but swirled her tongue in concert with his, as if their mouths were continuing the languid dance.

Her soft moan reverberated through his chest and heightened his need. He slid his palms down her back and drew her buttocks into his hardened manhood. With a stuttered breath, she pulled her lips away. "We must not."

"But ye want it as much as I." She couldn't stop. Not now.

Lady Howard inched toward the door. "Wanting and maintaining one's self-control are two separate things." She clasped his face between her hands and joined her mouth with his, again showing the depth of her passion. "Sleep well, Sir Alexander."

His entire body shuddered while he forced himself to inch away. She was right, but it took every ounce of Alex's strength to resist taking her into his arms and carrying her to the bedchamber. "Before I go, please tell me one thing."

The candlelight flickered amber in her eyes. "Yes?"

He licked his lips and glanced toward the coveted, yet sacrosanct bedchamber. "I would like to know the given name of the woman who can kiss me so passionately she makes me want to climb to the rooftops and roar."

Her cheeks turned the color of her mantle and she grasped the latch. "Jane," she whispered.

"Well then." He stepped in and touched his lips to her forehead. "Goodnight, Lady Jane."

Chapter Seven

Jane spent most of the morning tying bundles of rushes for the roof. Alexander had shown her how sennights ago, saying the roof repairs would proceed much faster if she tied the bundles while he finished up the fencing. She was delighted to help. It filled her with a sense of empowerment to take part in the repairs. When Mr. Cox returned, he would be immensely impressed with the amount of work she—actually they—had accomplished.

Mr. Cox? Jane straightened—goodness, she hadn't thought of the endearing valet in some time. *He should have paid a visit by now.* Had something happened at Buttermere Castle? She offered a silent prayer for his good health. But what if he was sick or injured? How would she obtain her supplies? Feeding Alexander, she would run out of wheat and oats soon.

Perhaps she'd mention it to Alexander. He might have a sensible suggestion. Jane cringed. Mr. Cox wouldn't like it when he saw the Scotsman, but she'd just have to make him understand Alexander posed no threat.

She craned her neck and searched for him, but the Highlander wasn't at the fence line. However, the sheep grazed nearby. The poor animals were looking more bedraggled by the day. Perhaps she should invite Alexander to dinner again so they could discuss the remaining work to be done as well as when he expected to take his leave.

In the past month, she'd grown accustomed to his presence. It pained her to think Alexander would be on his way. She'd even been sleeping better at night, knowing he was only a stone's throw away. Hopefully the roof would take at least another month—and then he'd need to repair the stable roof as well. That would detain him a bit longer. There would be weeding and planting, harvesting, wood to chop. Jane smiled. Living in the wild, there was no end to all the chores needing attention.

She tied off the last bit of twine and snipped it with the shears, then set out to find Alexander with Max happily trotting at her heel. Surprised not to see the Highlander in the paddock, she peeked inside the stable. *Odd.* "Alexander?"

The sound of water splashed at the rear of the building. *Ah, he must be cleaning the trough.*

She headed around back and abruptly stopped. Frozen in place, she couldn't breathe. Her mouth went dry, tingles skittered across her flesh. She'd never seen anything more beautiful in her life.

Completely naked, Alexander stood with his back to her.

Unable to turn away, Jane's gaze followed the dripping dark auburn locks to square and muscular shoulders. Sparkling with the afternoon sun, his back muscles bulged and rippled with his every move. Powerfully built beyond imagination, his shoulders tapered in a V to a lean waist. His hips, though narrow, supported chiseled buttocks, dimpled by muscular flesh. But his skin wasn't smooth. He was riddled with white and pink scars—a sure sign of a knight.

He splashed water under his arms, and it glistened down his back in streaks. Jane splayed her fingers. If only she could reach out and touch him. Swallowing against her arid throat, she stepped forward, her breaths stilted by staccato gasps.

Max raced ahead and bounded up behind Alexander. He turned. "Max…"

Further flummoxed, her gaze shot to his manhood. She clapped a hand over her mouth. Copper ringlets framed him. A fire ignited deep within her core, so hot, her body screamed for her to strip off her kirtle and bare her breasts to him. Never in her life had Jane experienced such wantonly desires, but in this moment, she coveted nothing more than to feel Alexander's body pressed to hers. She craved the experience of loving a man without fear of pain or retribution.

"Forgive me." Alexander reached for his plaid. "I thought I wouldna bother ye back here."

Jane's gaze slid up the undulating muscles of his abdomen to his potent chest, and finally met his humored gaze. She couldn't manage to utter a sound.

He covered himself. "Apologies. I've only one change of clothes, and they were getting on the nose. I daresay, I do no' ken how ye could stand to be around me."

Her breath caught. His chin shone smooth as silk. Without a word, she closed the gap and brushed her fingers along his jaw. "You shaved."

"Aye." He cleared his throat and his Adam's apple bobbed. "Ah. Did ye need me for something?"

She tried to stare at his face to avoid looking at his chest, heaving with his every breath. And for a moment, her mind went completely blank.

A sheep bleated.

Snapping to the present, she quickly turned her back as heat rushed to her cheeks. Had she honestly been ogling him? "Excuse my intrusion, Sir Alexander. I-I was wondering if we might do some shearing on the morrow?"

"'Tis a good idea. We should get an early start."

For some reason his voice sounded deeper. Jane clapped a hand to her chest to quell her rapid heartbeat. "Perhaps if you were to come inside for the evening meal we could discuss the work to be done. I realized this morning you've already been here longer than I…we had planned."

She glanced over her shoulder and he stepped nearer. *Heaven, give my boneless limbs strength.*

"Aye, m'lady. On both accounts." He placed his hand on her shoulder—a simple gesture, yet Jane closed her eyes and leaned into him. "I am in no hurry to go, unless ye no longer wish for me to remain."

From the way her body trembled beneath his touch, it would be most prudent to send him on his way. "This evening, then?" Her words had a tremor.

He removed his hand and a chilly breeze filled its place. "Aye."

His voice had undeniably grown deeper.

Before she did anything else she would regret, Jane fled back to the cottage. Wringing her hands, she paced. Roderick had looked nothing like Alexander. In fact, she'd never seen her husband completely disrobed. She'd seen parts of him exposed, and that which she did see never caused any stirrings whatsoever. Mayhap before they were married, she'd had a stirring or two. Roderick did have a pleasing face, but he wasn't as powerfully built as Sir Alexander—not by half.

When he comes to dine, I must keep the Highlander at arm's length. She wouldn't don any finery at all this time. She would focus their discussion on work that needed to be done. Jane headed into her bedchamber and picked up a piece of vellum, a quill and ink. If she drew up a list, it would keep her mind off Sir Alexander's rough hands…and her completely unacceptable, ridiculous desire for him to place those hands upon her.

Beside the inkwell was a bolt of linen Mr. Cox had delivered with her trunk. Alexander said he only had one suit of clothes. Perhaps she should make a shirt for him? She was a good seamstress. Sewing was one of the few practical things she'd learned as the daughter of the Earl of Nottingham. Of course, most of her work was embroidery, but she could measure and cut a simple shirt, bar the neck and sleeve ruffles. If he wanted something fancy, he'd best go to a tailor.

But Jane knew Alexander well enough. He wouldn't care about ruffles or fine linen—not the way Roderick had. The earl had spent a great deal of coin and time ensuring he dressed in royal style, even though they resided in the far north of England.

She'd simply handcraft the shirt to show her appreciation for his hard work. She would then encourage him to return to Scotland. If she ever again heard the sound of water splashing, she would turn and walk the other way. *Ogling a naked man? How could I have been so daft?*

By the time Alexander knocked on her door, Jane had her writing materials set out on the table, a string for measurements, kettle scones made and her nicest-tasting pottage yet simmered above the fire. She smoothed her hands over her skirt, stood tall and affected her best air of English indifference. Having spent the afternoon building her wall of resistance, nothing Sir Alexander possessed would knock it down.

Then she opened the door.

Had his eyes become a darker shade of blue since this morning when she'd found him completely bare? The image of his exquisite, naked body flooded back to the forefront of her memory with the force of a white-capped wave.

She stared. "Ah." How on earth could a man bathe and present himself upon her stoop as if he were a Greek god?

Alexander didn't move. Unquestionably, the color of his eyes had taken on a midnight hue. An unmistakable look of longing stretched his features.

They held each other's gazes.

Shivers coursed across Jane's skin, her heart thrumming a rapid beat. His lips parted as if he were going to speak. Stepping inside, he uttered not a word. The door closed behind him and before she could blink, the brawny Highlander swept her into his embrace.

Powerless to resist his advances, Jane's knees gave way as he crushed his mouth over hers. This wasn't a deep, exploring, sultry kiss. This was a claiming, fervent joining of the mouths that screamed, *I need more of you.* Ignited by a bone-melting fire that spread through her blood, she cupped his face with her hands and returned his ardent kisses whilst he carried her to the bedchamber.

"My God, Jane. Ye stir yearnings in me I never knew existed."

She panted. "You as well?" He rested her on the bed. Jane scooted to the edge. "But we cannot…"

His tongue shot out and moistened his lips. "Why? I ken the look in yer eye. I felt the passion behind yer kiss as well."

"Heaven's stars." Jane ran her trembling fingers over her hair. *Please kiss me again.* "Everything about you makes the blood course hot beneath my skin." She glanced aside. "Cou-could this be the work of the devil?"

"Nay." He grasped her hand and smiled—a devilish grin that made her head swoon. "A passion that grows between a man and a woman is a thing to be cherished. I did no' have it when I was married, and I suspect ye did no' as well."

He lowered his gaze to her breasts. His tongue sneaking to the corner of his mouth, he traced his finger across her exposed flesh. "Make love with me, Lady Jane."

The whispered words claimed her heart and transported her to a place with no shame. When she closed her eyes, a deep sigh escaped her lips. How could a rugged man's touch be so gentle and his deep voice send her insides into a maelstrom of flitting butterflies? Powerless to resist, she reached for his hand and kissed his open palm.

Chuckling, he unlaced her bodice and revealed the tops of her breasts. Jane couldn't think of her past—couldn't even remember it. Not now. Alexander pulled the ribbon on her shift and revealed her stays. Jane threw her head back as he fluttered kisses over her tingling flesh. His tongue shot beneath her bindings and found her nipple. "I need to taste ye."

Oh God, yes.

He helped her shrug out of her kirtle, and when she stood, the gown cascaded to the floor. He made quick work of unlacing her stays and casting them aside. Wearing only her shift, she tugged his shirt up from under his belted plaid. "I want to see you bare again." She didn't care how brazen she sounded—her whole body was afire with desire.

His white teeth sparkled with that devilish grin. He whipped the linen over his head and kicked off his boots.

Barely able to keep her hands steady, Jane reached for his plaid and tugged. "May I?"

He nodded.

She unwrapped the wool twice, before it fell away and exposed all of him. In the candlelight, he was even more magnificent. With a deep growl, he inclined his head lower and captured her mouth. The hungry swipe of his tongue made the air whoosh from her lungs. His hard manhood ground into her abdomen. But she needed him lower.

A flicker in her mind reminded that she could conceive, but she dismissed it. After eight years of marriage, she'd remained barren. *I want him lower.*

His fingers clutched her shift, slowly drawing it up over her thighs. The anticipation drove her to the brink of shameless abandon. Jane craved for her bare skin to touch his.

When at last he pulled her shift all the way off, he cupped her breasts in his palms as if he were holding a tiny bird. "Ye are so fine, m'lady."

Jane's breath stuttered as he dipped his chin and suckled her. Wrapping her arms around his shoulders, she closed her eyes and moved her hips toward him, her body demanding more friction. While his tongue swirled around her nipple, Jane feared she might burst. Steeling her resolve, she took his hand and slid onto the bed. "I've never done this without being beaten first."

Alexander pulled back. Suddenly aware of her nakedness, Jane crossed her arms over her breasts.

"Nay." He climbed over her and gently tugged her arms away. "The act of lovemaking should never be done by force."

Unable to speak, she gazed into his storm-blue eyes and nodded. Heaven help her, she wanted this. Her past be damned.

He suckled her finger and then ran languid kisses all the way up her arm. His auburn locks had come loose from the thong and hung over one eye. He could ravish her with a look, and Jane could have begged him to do so.

He kissed her flesh all the way to her navel then grinned. "I'll wager ye've never been shown the depths of yer passion."

Jane had no idea what he meant until he coaxed her legs open with his shoulders. *Oh Mother Mary, he wants to kiss me there too?* "No!"

He looked up and winked. "Just close yer eyes and let me take ye to heaven."

Jane tried to relax. He flicked his tongue across her womanhood. Gasping, her thighs quivered with need. Heat churned deep inside her body as her mind pictured the length of his manhood. She couldn't keep her eyes closed. She had to watch him.

Glory be, he'd meant what he said about heaven. Alexander's tongue worked magic and Jane was powerless to stop him. She grasped the bedclothes in her fists and gave in to his wicked licks while she watched him. Her breath sped. She cried out. All at once she could take no more. With a burst of euphoria, the world shattered around her. Tossing her head from side to side, perspiration at her temples, Jane's body pulsated as never before.

When at last her breathing slowed, Alexander rested on his side and nuzzled into her hair. "Was it good for ye, lass?"

Oh, how she could listen to that alluring brogue forever. "Yes," she whispered. His manhood pressed into her hip and she cast her gaze downward. Her shameless need ignited inside again. "But not for you."

"I gain me pleasure from watching ye come undone."

She rolled to her side and grasped his manhood in her palm. "Do you like it when I touch you?" Her fingers gripped lightly as she worked her hand along his shaft.

"Mm," he purred. "Verra much."

Lowering his lashes, his lips neared. Alexander's kisses were not as urgent, but the languid strokes of his tongue were all the more impassioned. She returned his kisses with fervor while gently stroking him. Her own desire leading her to the ragged edge yet again.

His warm hand cupped her breast. "I can hold back no longer."

Neither could she. Jane wanted to feel a man make love to her without being afraid. She'd lived eight and twenty years and had never known this kind of passion.

Alexander climbed between her legs, his member swollen and rigid as a sword. "Are ye ready for me?"

Too overcome to speak, Jane nodded, reached down and guided him. With his first thrust he filled her. She gasped repeatedly while he slowly slid her length. Once they were completely joined, a satisfied moan rumbled through his chest.

Jane had never been so alive, so willing to give herself to another. Alexander rocked his hips, slid in and out in a steady rhythm. With mounting friction, her thighs trembled again. Together they rode the wave of passion until once more she cried out and gasped for breath. Alexander sped the pace while she quivered around him. After one deep thrust, he held his body taut, threw back his head and roared.

***

Alex languished with Jane in his arms, allowing himself to savor their lovemaking. Having slept on the stable floor for a month, the feather down in Lady Jane's mattress cradled him as if he were floating on a cloud. Even better, the woman who'd consumed his every waking thought lay with her locks of tawny hair sprawled across his chest.

She trailed her fingers along his belly and made gooseflesh rise upon his skin. "Why are you still here?" she asked, her soft voice curious, rather than accusing.

The past came back to him so quickly, his every muscle grew tense. "Ye've needed me." It wasn't the full truth, but they both knew that.

"Yes, I have." She rested her warm palm on his chest. "But your wounds are long past healed. You have your bow and arrows. You could have set out and returned to your people sennights ago, but still you chose to stay."

He smoothed a hand over her silken tresses. "I agreed to remain here to help ye until the work is done."

"Mm hmm." She nuzzled into him. "But there's more."

He'd told her he had sailed from his home after Ilysa's death. But they'd both agreed not to talk about their pasts. Lady Jane had some dark secret she couldn't reveal. Alexander's story was grim, though everyone on Raasay knew of it.

They lay quietly in each other's arms for a time.

"Where are you from in the Highlands?" she asked.

Why not tell her? "Raasay—a small island nestled between the Isle of Skye and the mainland."

"Is it nice there?"

"Aye, lass. The keep presides over the Inner Sound of Raasay, and seals swim onto our shores." He exhaled. "'Tis isolated, like a wee kingdom."

She sighed dreamily. "It sounds delightful."

"It was. Once."

With a catch of her breath, her acorn eyes met his. "Why no longer?"

The searing pain in his heart spread throughout his chest while a lump the size of an apple swelled in his throat. "Ilysa's death was me own fault." He clenched his fist and shook it. "If I'd been a bit faster, I would have saved her."

"You feel responsible?"

"I *am* responsible."

Silence filled the chamber while Alexander's mind recounted the events from the most horrid day in his miserable life. He clutched his arm around Jane's shoulders and stared at the rafters above. "Ye asked me why I chose to stay. Aye, ye need me help. But I cannot think of returning home and facing me clan—or walking along the battlements and passing the crenel notch where Ilysa fell. She'd climbed up to watch the seals play on Brochel beach—half the clan was there making merry. I do no' even ken how it happened."

"It was something very bad, wasn't it?" Jane whispered.

He sucked in a hissing breath. "Ilysa screamed. I lunged and reached for her, but the lassie's hand slipped just beyond me grasp."

"She fell?"

He opened his fingers and stared at his palm. "Aye. Two hundred feet to the rocky crag below."

Jane's body curled into him. "Dear Lord, how devastating."

Alexander closed his eyes and swallowed. Hard. Then he drew in a stuttered breath. "I must head home soon, for I left me wee bairn in the care of me mother's arms."

Jane lifted her head and looked him in the eye. "You have a child?"

"Aye, Malcolm, me heir." Alexander ran his fingers through Lady Jane's hair and inhaled her God-given scent. "Me mother's the daughter of the Earl of Southampton. 'Tis why I ken yer bred of nobility."

Chapter Eight

Ian MacLeod sat on the dais in Brochel Castle's great hall and listened to the last supplication of the day. The blacksmith and the farrier couldn't come to terms on the number of horseshoes that had been made or used. Ian wasn't sure which. He had no idea how his brother and his father before him could listen to driveling complaints twice per week. And with the opposing information presented by each side, it was obvious neither party would be satisfied with a compromising outcome.

Hamish, the smithy, stretched his arms to his sides. "Ye shod every horse in the stable, plus the crofters. Ye took eighty shoes."

"Ye're a bloody thief as well as daft. I used half that," said Simon, the self-righteous farrier.

"Then where's me wrought iron gone? Got up and walked out the smithy shop on its own, has it?" Hamish leaned in and shook his finger. "Explain that."

Simon stepped into the accusing finger. "I'm no' responsible for yer miserable iron."

Ian rolled his eyes toward Sir Bran. The MacLeod henchman stood to his right and looked as irritated as Ian's gut felt. "Stop." Ian sliced his hand through the air. "How much wrought iron is missing?"

Hamish scratched his thick beard. "A stone, I'd reckon."

Ian leaned forward. "How much would seven pounds cost ye?"

"Four pennies, m'laird."

Though he was acting laird, Ian preferred to be called sir. His brother was laird, and he hoped to God Alexander would return to Brochel soon. "Very well, the MacLeod coffers will make up half yer losses." Ian looked to the farrier. "Simon, pay Hamish one penny and the smithy will take the loss for the other."

Hamish stepped forward. "But—"

Ian stood and fisted his hips. "That is all I will hear on the matter. Now be gone with ye and yer petty grievances."

The double doors to the great hall opened with a whoosh and in strode William, Clan MacLeod's most trusted messenger.

Ian beckoned him forward and raised his voice. "What news?" He shot a grimace toward Bran. "It had best be good."

By the guarded expression on William's face, Ian harbored little hope they'd found Alexander. *Blast.*

The messenger walked straight to the dais. "No one's seen him. 'Tis as if he vanished."

Ian refused to believe it. "Not in Glasgow or Edinburgh?"

"Nay, not a sign."

"What about Harris or all the Hebrides?" Bran asked.

"Nay." William spread his palms. "And we nearly got our throats cut when we dropped anchor at Lewis."

"God's teeth, will it never end? Uncle Ruairi is still up to his ruthless tricks." Ian paced. "Did ye try Inverness?"

"Aye, and nay, he's no' up north, he's no' in the Orkneys or the Shetlands."

Frowning, Bran crossed his arms over his mammoth chest. "Iona?"

"The abbey?" William threw his hands out to his sides. "Now that's pushing it a bit, but, nay. He's no' there either."

Ian wasn't about to let it rest. "Did ye sail the Firth of Solway?"

"Nay." William dragged his fingers through his hair. "Bloody hell, dunna ye remember ye told me to go no further than the Mull of Galloway afore I reported back?"

Bran pulled out a chair and slumped into it. "Did ye show everyone the drawing?"

"Aye." William's voice rose. "Nary a bloody soul in the Kingdom of Scotland has seen a wee *birlinn* with dragons' heads at her bow and stern."

Ian pounded his fist on the table. "I'll be a mangled fool-born bastard."

"Just who do you say is fool-born?" Lady Anne asked, walking from the stairwell. Perched upon her hip was Ian's nephew, Malcom, the MacLeod of Raasay heir.

Ian ground his teeth, but held out his hands and kissed his mother on the cheek. "Good morrow, ma."

"Good morrow." She didn't smile and handed the babe to Ian. "What news of my eldest son?"

Malcom gurgled and placed his little palms on Ian's face. Ian loved the bairn, but presently had no time to act as nursemaid. "No sightings."

"Yet," Bran said.

"Aye." Ian gave Malcom a wee pinch on his chubby cheek and set the toddler on the floor. He wasn't about to accept that the lad might be an orphan. He looked to William and Bran. "We'll extend our search. William, ye and John sail the *Flying Swan* to Ireland. Bran and I will take *The Golden Sun* and sail the English coast—we may need the bigger guns there." Ian turned to Lady Anne and placed a hand on her shoulder. "Ye'll have to manage as laird in our absence."

She gave him a somber nod. "I had to run the castle when you were but a lad every time your father sailed on his *privateering* voyages. I may be older, but I can still issue orders."

Ian liked his mother's spirit. "Ye'll have Merrin to help ye with Malcom."

Bran stepped beside them. "Enya and our brood will do anything for ye, of course."

Lady Anne's brow furrowed beneath her grey wimple. She grasped Ian's arm, her eyes pleading. "Just find my son. Tell him he has a child at home who needs a father."

"Aye," Ian said. "And a clan who needs his leadership."

***

Jane snipped the thread and held up the finished shirt. *I say, it looks as if it was made by a tailor.* Standing, she hummed a merry tune and twirled across the floor with the shirt in her arms. The past sennight had been the happiest of her life. Alexander embodied everything she'd missed from her marriage to Roderick. Jane lightly brushed her fingers over the tops of her breasts. Nightly, Alex had shown her a new facet of the tenderness that could exist between a man and a woman. She'd never guessed a lady could enjoy such unbridled passion behind the closed doors of a bedchamber.

And to think she'd found love isolated in the wilderness. Her unbounded happiness was nothing short of a miracle. She twirled back the other way and Max yipped, wagging his tail. "Come along, boy. Let us go find Sir Alexander."

She chuckled while she skipped into the yard with Max close behind. Alexander had fashioned a ladder, which was pitched against the roof. She stood back and shaded her eyes with her hand. *My, he's made quite a bit of progress since morning.* He used strips of leather he'd cut from pigskin to tie the thatch bundles in place. She stood for a moment and admired him, broad shoulders, powerful legs, skirted by plaid. Simply looking at the man made her blood run hot.

Jane flapped the shirt through the air. "I do believe 'tis time for your nooning," she hollered.

Alexander looked her way and grinned. Jane's heart thrummed, sending her insides aflutter. Hewn of pure muscle, rugged as the tallest pine in the forest, his smile was the most devilish thing about him. He made her turn wanton with that grin.

"Ye finished it, did ye?"

"Yes, now come down and try it on."

Had she not been intimate with Alexander, watching him descend the ladder would have made her blush clear down to the tips of her toes. His kilt flicked up, giving her a pleasing eyeful of chiseled derriere. Making him a pair of braises crossed her mind, but she discounted the idea. That simply would not do.

"Are you hungry?" she asked when he hopped off the last rung, unable to hide her shameless grin.

He brushed her cheek with the back of his knuckle. "Aye. A bit of venison would be tasty on one of yer kettle scones."

"At least your stomach is predictable, because that's exactly what we're having." She grasped his hand and led him into the cottage whilst holding up the shirt. "But first, try on my masterpiece."

Alexander reached for the shirt and held it up. He closely examined the seams and gave them a good tug. "Sewn sturdy, just like a Highland tailor would do." He smoothed his fingers around the neckline and hummed appreciatively. "Better, mayhap."

Jane clapped. "Do you really like it?"

He glanced down at his dirty shirt, now sporting two holes, one atop the other. "Aye, lass."

She rolled her hands through the air. "Well then, try it on."

Alexander shrugged out of the old rag and pulled the clean linen garment over his head.

"Oh my." Jane studied the form beneath. How utterly masculine he made the bit of fabric appear. Her tongue slipped to the corner of her mouth and she tugged at the shoulder seams. "Not too tight?"

He stretched his arms forward. "Nay. It fits like it was made for me."

She gave him a playful thwack. "It was."

He slid his hands around her waist and kissed her. "My thanks. I shall always wear this shirt with fond memories."

Jane swallowed against the lump forming in her throat. She hadn't thought about Alexander's eventual departure in some time. She pretended to fuss over the cuff. "What is your clan like?"

"Och, MacLeods are made of solid stock."

"Like you?"

"I suppose. They eke out a living, tilling the rocky soil on Raasay. Me da did plenty to help the clan through a length of difficult times."

Jane ran her finger up his arm. "Since your mother was the daughter of an earl, was your father nobly born?" They both had been so secretive about their pasts, she'd been seeking a way to ask Alex this question without bringing to the focus upon her state of affairs.

Alexander looked toward the door and sighed. "Aye, me da was the first MacLeod Chieftain of Raasay."

Her finger continued up and traced the stubbled line of his chin. "Are you a laird, Alexander?" she asked with a breathless whisper.

A muscle in his jaw twitched, but he said nothing. Jane looked him in the eye and arched a single brow.

"Aye." His admission was barely audible.

Jane's smile dropped. She tactfully twirled out of his arms, picked up the knife and started carving the venison. Two dreadful thoughts warred inside her tightening chest. The one thing she'd feared since the day he arrived was that his clan wouldn't rest until they found him, and if they arrived upon her doorstep, her hiding place would be revealed. Worse, she couldn't bear the thought of losing him. In a short time, Alexander had consumed her every thought. It had been so wonderful to have a man, a companion at the cottage. Moreover, he provided much more interesting conversation than Max, and he spoke to her as an equal. No man had ever conversed with her thus.

She placed a slice of meat on a trencher. Since Alexander was a Highland chieftain, she could not entertain dreams of having him stay—and he'd mentioned he had an heir. When would he grow tired of her company and set out?

Jane's neck burned when he came up behind her. "Ye've grown suddenly quiet."

She set the knife down and pressed the heel of her hand to her eyes. "What if your clansmen come looking for you? They may bring locals with them."

"If they venture this far south, I doubt they'd give a wee village like St. Bees a cursory glance."

She chewed the inside of her cheek. "What about a port town? Whitehaven, for example?"

Alexander nodded and swiped his hand down his chin. "Aye, across the Firth of Solway from the Mull of Galloway wouldna be out of the question."

"Whitehaven is only four miles northeast of Abbey Wood."

He got that faraway look in his eye again and smirked. "I cannot believe I did no' ask ye when I first arrived—I'd just assumed St. Bees was a heathen village separated from civilization by leagues."

She pretended to straighten his shirt's collar. "Why do you think you chose not to ask?"

"I suppose it did no' matter. I needed a place to lick me wounds." He brushed his finger along her cheek. "And I did no' see fit to leave just yet." His voice grew husky and his fan of long lashes shuttered his blue eyes.

Jane's stomach erupted in a maelstrom of butterflies as his mouth neared. If only she could envelop him in her arms and hold him there forever. His lips caressed hers with a tingling rush of gooseflesh as if it were their first. Alex deepened his kiss with a moan, molding his body to hers. She may not be able to hold this man in her arms forever, but she would relish every single moment they shared together.

Alexander rested his forehead against hers. "What about ye, m'lady? What brought ye here to Abbey Wood and why are ye so afraid of being discovered?"

Her gut clamped into a solid ball. Jane stepped back and clasped her hands under her chin. "Oh no, we agreed. I cannot...can *never* speak of it."

He knitted his brows. "But that was afore we knew each other."

Jane shook her head. "No, no, no."

Alexander clapped his hands to his hips. "God's teeth. I've poured me heart out, revealed all about me past—something I never thought I'd do." He combed his fingers through his hair. "We've been intimate, yet ye will no' open up to me."

She scooted away, her palms wet with perspiration. "Why can you not understand?"

A loud knock resounded on the door. "Lady Whitehaven?"

Alexander flinched. "*Who?*" he mouthed.

Jane's head spun. *Of all the bad timing.* "Mr. Cox!" The pitch of her voice rose as high as a meadowlark.

Chapter Nine

Jane cleared her throat, stood tall and opened the door with a practiced smile. "Mr. Cox. I was beginning to wonder if something had happened to you."

The old man beamed, a grin spread across his careworn face. "I cannot believe all the changes you have made. I never would have thought you capable, my lady, but give you a few weeks of fine weather, and the fencing is done, the roof work is underway."

"Um." Jane stole a glance at Alexander and bit her lip. She couldn't very well keep the Highlander hidden. And it would take to the count of three before Mr. Cox realized she'd had help. She moved aside and beckoned him inside. "Please, come in."

Bundles of supplies in hand, he stepped across the threshold. "I had no idea a noblewoman would be so learned in such matters…" He glanced at the dirty shirt draped over the chair. Thick eyebrows flew up in concert with an alarmed grimace spreading across his face.

Alexander folded his arms and frowned.

Regarding the Highlander, Mr. Cox dropped his parcels and blanched. "Holy Mary, Mother of God." The dread in his voice sounded as if the world had come to an end.

Jane hastened beside Alexander. "Look what blew in with that nasty storm we had the last time you were here."

The old man's color changed from white as bed linen to scarlet. He glared at Alex, his steely eyes forming a hateful squint.

Jane emitted a nervous laugh. "This is…ah…Alexander from Scotland. He's been staying in the stable. He ran into some trouble and managed to collapse upon my threshold."

Mr. Cox blanched. "He's been here over a month?"

"Yes…"

Alexander stepped forward. "Aye. The place was crumbling around the lady's ears. I'd have been no kind of gentleman if I did no' help her ladyship fix a few things lest she end up without shelter."

Mr. Cox glanced at Jane with disbelief, drawing his jowls into a glower. "I give you a place to stay and you invite a barbarian, not only onto the property, but inside the cottage without so much as an escort?"

"Mr. Cox!" Jane stamped her foot. "I believe you've overstepped your station." Yes, the old man had been inordinately kind, but he was a servant accusing her of impropriety. She gestured to Alexander. "This poor man's boat was capsized in St. Bees. He was robbed by the local thieves and beat half to death. Whilst he's been convalescing, he has been exceedingly selfless, making repairs to *your* cottage, which would have taken me months, if not years to complete."

Alexander held up his hands. "I must say leaving a noblewoman in the wild to fend for herself is akin to negligence."

"*Me?* Negligent?" The old man's lips thinned as he stepped toward Alex. "And who do you think you are, a Highlander coming to *my* family's home and making yourself cozy?"

Towering over Mr. Cox, Alexander planted his fists on his hips. "Me name's Alexander MacLeod, Second Chieftain of Clan MacLeod of Raasay, and I do no' take kindly to a fella who is both remiss *and* ungrateful when a man's toiled with his bare hands and fixed up yer shabby hovel at no expense to yerself!"

"You, sir, are a reprehensible tinker and a reiver if I ever saw one. No fancy Scottish titles carry any weight this side of the border." Mr. Cox's complexion took on an even deeper shade of red. He snatched Jane's arm and tugged her to the far end of the room. "This man could ruin everything for you," he whispered, cupping his hand over his mouth so not to be heard. "My lady, you know as well as I, it could mean you *burn*."

Jane stole a panicked glance at Alexander. Standing across the room with his arms folded, he looked as if he could grab Mr. Cox by the scruff of the neck and toss him clear to the next shire. "He shan't reveal…"

The old man shook his knotty finger. "Mark me, I come to tell you the new Earl of Whitehaven has tasked the sheriff with tracking your whereabouts. You simply cannot take in vagrants, even if they are able to repair the roof."

Jane tugged her arm from his grasp and moved toward Alexander. "Mr. Cox, please be reasonable."

"Have you lost your mind?" Cox shouted. Grimacing, he bowed depreciatively. "*My lady*, excuse my impertinence, but I have treated you with utmost respect. Nonetheless, this man must leave *my* cottage at once."

"I ken when I'm no' wanted—and I ken when I've been played for a fool." His icy stare scorched Jane's skin. Alex pushed past her and headed toward the door. "Damn yer secrets. I've heard enough."

"Alexander!" Jane jumped when the door slammed behind his retreating form. Pursing her lips, she addressed Mr. Cox with fists clenched. "Have you forgotten your station? Yes, I am indebted to you for the use of this cottage, but your treatment of Laird Alexander is deplorable."

Mr. Cox's shoulders dropped with his sigh. "Forgive me, my lady, but I haven't gained an opportunity to spirit away from Buttermere Castle because of increased suspicion. 'Tis as if the new Lord of Whitehaven will not rest until you are abducted and punished for your crime."

Jane turned toward the hearth and drew her hands over her hair. "My heavens, will it never end?"

"Who knows, but the servants are on edge. The earl has increased the guard and put the sheriff in charge of his army. We're all being watched as if every one of us conspired to murder Lord Roderick."

"'Tis that bad?" Her gut clenched. "I cannot bear to have you or any of the servants suffering on my account."

"I hope things will calm down once the earl finds other matters with which to concern himself." He pressed his palms together as if he were praying. "Please, I beg of you. Allow no one else on the property and keep yourself hidden. With any luck, the Highlander will collect his things and head straight to Scotland without revealing your whereabouts."

Jane clutched her arms across her body. "I believe Laird Alexander to be trustworthy."

"I pray to God he is, but his very presence here is a threat. What if he brings more smelly Scots from the Highlands upon us? You shall be discovered." His head shook with his foreboding inhale. "On that there is no doubt."

"He said his clan wouldn't be looking for him. He lost his wife—needed some time away…"

"Let us pray he speaks the truth." Mr. Cox gestured to the parcels on the floor. "I've brought your supplies. I have no idea when I'll be able to return." He bowed. "Godspeed, my lady."

Jane barely heard him. Alexander couldn't simply walk out of her life. Her throat constricting, she accompanied Mr. Cox to the door. Her hands grew clammy. She'd had a brief respite from danger, from living in fear, but now her plight returned with full force.

She dipped her head toward Mr. Cox respectfully. "My thanks for your continued generosity."

He offered a bow. Jane stood on the threshold and watched the valet mount his horse and head to the overgrown path.

A clatter came from the stable. Jane rushed out of the house and around the back. *Mr. Cox's timing couldn't have been worse.*

Alexander had donned his doublet and had his bow and a quiver of arrows over his shoulder. He stopped and stared at her, his eyes determined and intense.

Max came from nowhere and rubbed against her leg. She slapped her hand to her chest, attempting to dislodge the lump in her throat. "Are you leaving?" *Please no. Don't do this to me.*

"Aye, the master of this cottage made his wishes clear."

She drew in a ragged breath. "Mr. Cox is only worried about me." She stepped forward and touched Alexander's elbow. "Stay…please…I cannot bear to see you go."

His lips thinned as he glanced away. "We both knew this day would come. The MacLeod probably thinks me dead by now and I've a son who needs his da." Alexander started for the path.

Jane grasped her skirts and kept pace with him. "Please. Stay just a little longer. I know you must return to your son. But I need you as well."

"Oh, *Lady Whitehaven*?" He turned on his heel and faced her. "Why couldna ye tell me ye were a countess? Do ye have any claim to the name Howard?"

"On that I did not lie, factually. 'Tis my father's family name." She clutched her fingers around his arm. "Can you not understand? I needed to conceal my identity…"

He tugged away. "Even after we made love? Even after I poured out me own despicable transgressions, ye cannot trust me?"

She gaped. Heaven's stars, he already knew too much. If she told him she'd taken Roderick's life to save her own, he could march into Whitehaven and reveal her hiding place. "I do trust you."

"Then what is this big secret ye have?" He strode off then stopped again. "God bless it, Jane. If ye cannot trust me by now, ye never will. Love cannot grow when there are dark secrets simmering below the surface of one's heart."

She spread her arms and took a step toward him. "But I do lo—"

He sliced his hand through the air. "Do no' say it. I'd take ye with me, but ye've proved yer feelings are nay as deep as mine." He picked up the dog and shoved him into Jane's arms. "Take Max into the house and do no' allow him to follow me."

"That's it, then? You're walking away?"

"I'm doing what I should have done near a month ago." He inched backward. "I'll nay forget ye, but we've lives to live. Our paths never should have crossed." The muscles in his jaw tightened and he bowed his head. "I wish ye well, m'lady."

She could utter not a sound, her throat raw, the pain in her chest unbearable. *This cannot be happening.* Jane blinked and a tear streamed down her face while she watched Alexander disappear into the wood. Dumbfounded, she stood for a moment, willing him to come back, staring at the thick foliage. The sound of his footsteps snapping twigs was soon replaced by bird whistles and the soft rustle of leaves.

He'd left her.

With Max in her arms, she staggered into the cottage. A wail burst through her throat as she set the dog down. *My God, I will never find happiness again.*

Fleeing to the bedchamber, she threw herself onto the bed and buried her face in the pillow. Why must life be fraught with suffering? Why could happiness only be fleeting glimpses in time? Why could Alexander not understand how much courage it had taken to allow him into her life? Some things could *never* be uttered. Never.

She rolled to her side and clutched the pillow to her breast. Rocking, Jane tried to suppress the pain tearing her heart to shreds.

***

Alexander marched through the forest like a wounded bull. God's teeth, what the hell had he been thinking? When he left Raasay, he'd been blinded by remorse and somehow Lady Jane had wound her English talons around his heart. He had no business staying in Abbey Wood, hiding from the world. Thankfully the pompous Mr. Cox came when he did. It was the blow to the gut Alex needed.

The further he walked from Jane's cottage, the more his mind honed. Finally, he had clarity of thought. Alex blinked and saw Malcom's cherubic face. His heart ached to again cradle the bairn in his arms. His life at Brochel Castle boiled to the surface. Oh, how he missed Ian and his mother. How he missed the familiar faces of his clan and the gatherings in the great hall.

Alex stopped when he arrived at the edge of Abbey Wood. In the distance, two men tilled a field. When they spotted him, one pointed.

Alexander had no time for a confrontation with any numbskull from St. Bees. He took a sharp turn and headed northeast toward Whitehaven. There would be a greater opportunity to find work in a port town. Perhaps with luck, he'd locate a transport headed to Scotland, else he might earn a few shillings working as a seaman so he could pay his way home. He snorted. Having been the master on many voyages, doing the work of an able seaman would take him back to his boyhood when he climbed the rigging for his father.

By the time Alexander walked onto the pier in Whitehaven, his mind had again run amuck with thoughts of Lady Jane. Heaven help him, he'd never had feelings for a woman like his craving for her. None too soon would he forget the depth of her acorn eyes, or the soft tresses that swept across his chest when they lay together.

But they were from different worlds. He doubted Jane would ever want to live in Scotland. Aye, being isolated in the wood was like living in a dream. It could never have lasted. Sooner or later they would be forced to interact with the locals, and that would be the end of their peace and quiet for good. Mr. Cox would protect Lady Jane until she gained a pardon from whatever crime she'd committed. Alex clenched his fists. He must cease worrying about her.

But he couldn't suppress his errant thoughts. The lady was so helpless, and that damned dog was of no use at all aside from companionship. While he walked, Alexander's gut twisted in knots no matter how he tried to justify his decision to leave.

When at last a familiar scene played out on the busy pier, he steeled his resolve. It was time to return home. A grand galleon sat at anchor in the bay—as handsome as his own ship, *The Golden Sun*. Two single-masted galleys and a double-masted barque bobbed in the waves, tied to mooring posts. A squire dressed in knee-length breeches, carrying rolls of parchment hastened past. Alexander held out his hand and stopped him. "Excuse me, sir."

The man took one look at Alexander's worn plaid and frowned. "Yes?"

"Would ye ken if any of these vessels is heading to Scotland?"

He pointed his thumb over his shoulder, toward the galleon. "The *St. Mary* is off to London once she's loaded. Don't know about the others—they're fishing boats, mainly."

"My thanks."

Alexander took in a deep inhale. Ah, the familiar smells of the sea—some pleasant, the dead fish floating near the shore unpleasant. He watched a pair of seamen struggle to roll a barrel up the gangway of one of the galleys. With a bit of training, the lads would have no trouble maneuvering the kegs on their own.

Alexander sauntered forward and tested a barrel sitting on the back of a horse-drawn cart. The contents inside sloshed, emitting an unmistakable aroma of hops. *Ale for certain.* Having spent the past month or so hauling logs and fallen trees for Lady Jane, Alexander took a chance. When a man needed employment, he must make a lasting impression. It took two Englishmen to push a barrel of ale up a wee gangway? Tugging down his shirt, Alex aimed to prove the might of a Scotsman.

Hefting the barrel over his shoulder, he drew in a couple quick inhales and steadied himself. Bloody hell, the blasted thing weighed more than he'd guessed. Clenching his teeth, his legs quivered with each step, but in no way would Alex let on how much the weight strained him. When he placed his foot on the gangway, he leaned forward to gain balance upon the slanted incline. He glanced up. Sailors from the galley were lined along the rail watching him.

"You drop that in the drink and I'll take the payment out of your hide." Those words must have come from the captain.

Alex tried to keep his face from grimacing. The damned barrel teetered precariously on his shoulder. He reached the top of the gangway, met by two seamen who helped him lower it. "My thanks," he said.

One gave him a nod. "I wouldn't want to see it take a tumble and crack the hull."

Brushing off his hands, Alex grinned. "Who said I aimed to let it fall?" He glanced around and spotted the captain. Dressed in a finely tailored doublet with a velvet bonnet, the man sauntered forward. "You took a mighty big risk with the men's ale."

Alex shrugged. "No' so much. I could have taken the barrel up a gangway twice as long, or seen it rigged and hoisted aboard a tall ship."

"You've experience, I take it?"

"Aye, raised on the sea. Just like any Scotsman from the Hebrides." Alexander reached for a length of rope and tied off a pair of bowline knots as if he could do it in his sleep. "I'm looking to earn me way home."

"Scotland?" The captain batted his hand through the air. "This boat fishes English waters. I've no taste for bloody Highland pirates raiding my ship."

Alexander smirked. *Smart fella.* "All I ask is a chance to earn me keep. I can navigate, man an oar, work the sail. In fact, there's no' a job on a galley I havena done."

The captain eyed him then squeezed Alexander's shoulder. "You have some muscle under that fine linen shirt, but I do not need another hand."

Alexander stood firm. "Give me a sennight. If I havena proved me worth by then, send me on me way, else pay a respectable wage and I'll ensure ye nay regret it."

The captain folded his arms and tilted up his chin. "Very well. I'll allow one turn at sea. And I'll not pay you a farthing if you turn out to be a lazy bastard."

Chapter Ten

After anchoring *The Golden Sun* in the Maryport harbor on the English side of the Firth of Solway, Ian and Bran took a half-dozen guardsmen ashore in a skiff. Ian clutched the scroll with the drawing of Alexander's *birlinn* under his arm. They were in hostile waters now. They'd stay to the waterfronts of each village, ask their questions and be on their way—as long as no one picked a fight.

Just in case that happened, every man was armed with a dirk in his belt, a claymore strapped to his back and daggers hidden in every known and unknown crevice of his kit.

Once they alighted at the pier, Sir Bran strode on Ian's right. Flanked by the guardsmen, there was little possibility they'd see trouble, but Ian didn't discount it either. He gave the bustling activity a careful inspection. Ahead, a clerk recorded goods being offloaded from a galley. Ian pointed. "There. He looks like the type of fella who'd notice everything."

"Aye," Bran agreed.

Ian led the group toward the man. "Hail, friend."

The clerk glanced up and paled, his gaze drifting to their weaponry. "You have business in Maryport, Highlander?"

Ian unrolled the velum. "We're looking for a *birlinn*." He held it out. "'Tis somewhat small, and unique in that it has dragons' heads at its stern and bow."

The man studied the drawing and then glanced sidewise. "I'm not certain."

Bran leaned in and cracked his knuckles. "What do ye mean? Ye've either seen the wee boat or nay."

The blighter rubbed his fingers together. "A shilling for my purse might help my memory."

Ian sneered. "Ye've got cods, blackmailing the lot of us."

"Perhaps, but there's nary a man on this pier who wouldn't fight for me, should I be threatened." He leaned forward on his perch. "You're not threatening me, are you, gentlemen?"

Ian dug in his sporran. This was most likely the first of many bribes he'd pay on this voyage. "Here's yer coin. Now, where have ye seen me *birlinn*?"

The clerk glanced over each shoulder. "There was a boat with dragons' heads like your drawing moored at this very pier a few sennights ago—they were selling their catch." He thumped his chest. "Everything that comes into Maryport must go through me. I collect the port taxes and direct the sailors to the merchants."

"What do ye mean, *they*?" Ian asked.

The man scratched his chin. "The crew, and I'll say, a bedraggled lot they were."

Bran's brows drew together. "Was there a Scotsman with them?"

"I do not recall." He twisted his mouth and drummed his fingers. "Come to think of it, the fishermen I saw were Englishmen. I thought it a bit odd considering they sailed a Highland *birlinn*. 'Tis rare to see vessels like that around these parts."

Ian's gut clenched as his gaze met Bran's. A tempest raged behind the henchman's dark stare. "I smell a rat." Ian glanced back to the clerk. "Where did these men hail from?"

"They didn't say." He shrugged. "I just record the goods and take tax payments."

Bran placed his giant hands on the wee table—he had an inimitable way of making a man nervous. "Where do ye *reckon* they hailed from?"

"I…" The man scooted backward. "I'd say east of here. If I recall correctly, they said something about having tried to sell their catch in St. Bees. Though I've no idea why anyone would bother sailing ashore there. The place is run by thieves." He held up his hand. "If you'll excuse me, I have work to do."

Ian inclined his head toward *The Golden Sun*. "Come, men. Let's away to the navigation room and set our course."

***

The sail picked up the wind as the English galley left the Port of Whitehaven while the crew manned the oars. Under the canopy at the bow, Alexander studied nautical maps. "If ye head for the reef off the Isle of Man, ye're sure to find cod."

The captain's grin twisted. "And risk sinking my boat?"

Alex hovered over the map and pointed. "If ye drop anchor here, ye'll no' be swept toward the isle by the undertow." Since the captain had been willing to take him on, Alex had no qualms about sharing a family secret or two.

The captain looked closer and grinned. "The west side, you say? What about Irish pirates?"

Alexander shrugged. "'Tis why ye need a cannon on yer deck."

The captain gazed out over the Firth of Solway and pointed. "I'd do anything to have an eighteen-gun galleon like that one."

With a snap of his head, Alex hastened to the ship's rail. His heart pummeled his chest. He'd recognize *The Golden Sun* anywhere. Every morning at Brochel Castle, he arose and gazed down upon his most prized possession anchored in Brochel Bay. His father had captured the English racing galleon during a privateering mission off the coast of Southern England. "Do ye have a spyglass?" Alexander snapped.

The captain pulled the glass from his belt. "What is it?"

"I ken that ship." Alexander held it to his eye. Sailing due west, Ian and Bran stood at the helm. His heart twisted in a knot. *They're searching for me.*

"Should we be worried?" the captain asked.

Returning the spyglass, Alex shook his head. "'Tis a friendly vessel." Admitting he owned that coveted ship could buy a world of trouble.

The captain pointed. "How do you know it? I don't recall seeing that ship in these waters before."

Oh, she'd been there all right, but not of late. "I was a member of her crew once."

"Truly? What caused you to leave, seeking employment on my fishing galley?"

Alexander swiped his hand across his mouth. "A woman." That wasn't really a lie. His gaze swept back to *The Golden Sun.* If only the captain would alter his course and follow that ship. "How long do ye reckon we'll be out?"

"When the hold is full of fish, and before the catch rots."

"Three days?"

"Perhaps four."

Blast me rotten luck. Even if Ian was stopping at every port, he could be halfway down the coast by the time they returned.

***

Max sniffed the wild daisies while Jane pulled weeds around the rose bushes. In the two days since Alexander left, she had immersed herself in work. But nothing eased her pain. Ever since she'd left her father's castle, fear had governed her life. First, she'd been afraid of Roderick—terrified he might kill her.

She pulled on a big hawkweed but it wouldn't budge. With both hands, she gave it a good yank, the leaves breaking away from the root, sending her rocking back on her bottom. "Curses." She tossed the weed aside. It might have been for the best if her husband had killed her rather than the other way around. Now she lived in fear for her life. She'd enjoyed a glimpse of happiness when Alexander was there—she had even slept at night.

On accord of her own pigheadedness, there she was, once again alone, a highborn woman trained in frivolous pursuits such as languages, needlepoint and music, trying to fend for herself.

Max raised his head and looked toward the wood, his ears pricked. Jane followed his line of sight. A crow called and flew from the tops of the trees. Jane slapped a hand to her heart. *Why must I startle so easily?*

Max crept toward the trees and growled.

Jane's heart hammered. "What is it, boy?"

The dog launched into a cacophony of barking. Jane stood. "Come, Max." She ran toward the cottage, slapping her hip, praying the dog was behind her.

Heavy footsteps swished through the grass. Max emitted a hideous snarl then yelped. Jane looked back. The spaniel lay in a heap on the grass. "Max!" Jane sprinted to the dog's side.

Close on her heels, a smelly brute laughed. "Looks like we found a ripe one."

Gulping air, Jane dropped to her knees. Max raised his head and whimpered. She might cower in fear for herself, but when it came to her dog, she'd stand and fight.

A brutish arm wrapped around her waist and pulled her to her feet. "Not so fast, wench."

Twisting in his grasp, Jane gritted her teeth and slammed her elbow into the man's chest. "Unhand me, you brigand!" She recoiled to deliver a slap, but the brute caught both her wrists and twisted. Squealing with the pain, Jane nearly fell. Her wimple tumbled to the ground.

The man's grip held fast, but his eyes budged. "Bloody Christmas, 'tis Lady Whitehaven."

Jane froze. Though she wanted to scream, the cry stuck in her throat—she was too terrified to utter a sound. Heaven help her, this was the end.

"Are you jesting?" His accomplice stepped in beside him with a black-toothed grin. He pinched a bit of her kirtle and rubbed it between his fingers. "What say you? We come out here to see why the Highlander rose from the dead, and look what we find."

Jane clenched her stomach muscles against the sickly lump forming there. "Please." *Dear God, help me.* She drew in a staccato breath and tried to jerk away. "Leave me alone. You have no idea what you are doing."

The man's grip tightened. "There's ten pounds on your head—that's enough coin for Roger and me to retire for the rest of our days." Jane jolted as his fingers bored into her flesh. "Oh no, you're not going nowhere. Roger, get the rope. We're taking her straight to the sheriff afore she tries to stab us like she did Lord Whitehaven."

The more Jane fought, the tighter the man's grip became. Her gaze darted to Max. He still lay in the grass. Would Alexander burst through the wood and spirit her to Raasay? Why had she not told him about Roderick? All he ever asked from her was the truth. Why had she withheld it even after he'd proved trustworthy?

A tear trickled from her eye and her lips trembled.

Please, Alexander. Come back.

Chapter Eleven

When they rounded the St. Bees point, Ian saw it. Unbelievable. If he had ordered William to sail the shore of northwestern England, they would have spotted the blasted *birlinn* sennights ago. "Furl the sails and drop anchor!"

Bran stepped beside him. "It looks as if the crew's bringing in their catch."

Ian smoothed his palm over his dirk's pommel. "It may be their last."

"Do ye think he's there?"

A weight the size of an anchor dropped in Ian's gut. "I'll no' surmise. But I doubt they'll see another sunrise if they cannot tell us where Alexander is." He turned to the men. "I want two skiffs of fighting men lowered. Bring yer muskets and swords. The rest of ye, man the cannons. Set the sights on the beach and light the slow matches. This very well could be the fight of our lives."

"I doubt that," Bran mumbled.

Ian elbowed the henchman in the ribs. "Now's no' the time to let our guard down. If we're ready for a battle and it doesna come, then the men can have an extra tot of whisky when this is over."

Standing at the back of the skiff, Ian didn't take his eyes off the four men offloading Alexander's *birlinn,* irked that not a one of them was his brother. "Row faster."

A few of the locals came to watch. About a dozen men lined the shore, battleaxes and swords in hand.

"At least they're no' running," Bran said.

Ian clenched the fists resting on his hips. "They should be." He didn't wait for the men to pull the boat ashore, but stomped through the surf with Bran falling in beside him. They marched straight to the shabby fishermen. "Where's the man who owns this *birlinn?*"

"'Tis mine," said a pox-faced, sniveling maggot.

"Ye think I'm daft?" Ian sauntered up to him. "This is me brother's boat, clear as the pimple on yer ugly chin. Now I'm going to ask one more time. Where is he?"

The man spat in his face. Ian didn't flinch. Drool oozing down his cheek, in one move he snatched the bastard's arm, spun him around and slipped a dagger to his neck. "This could have been easier for ye," he growled in the man's ear.

Bran and the MacLeods drew their swords, but no one challenged. *Milk-livered swine.*

Ian pushed the knife hard enough to draw blood. "I'll ask each one of ye if ye ken where me brother is and if ye dunna answer, ye'll end up in hell with this blighter." Ian gripped the knife for the deathly cut.

The man in his arms stammered. "W-wait."

Ian twitched. "Where?"

"He came into St. Bees acting like he owned the place."

"Ye dunna say?" Bran stepped forward. "Alexander MacLeod is more a gentleman than the lot of ye combined."

"Was," said a bent old woman from the crowd. Using a cane, she hobbled forward and pointed a gnarled finger at the man with Ian's knife at his neck. "I knew your evil deeds would come back to you, Willis."

The hackles on Ian's neck stood on end. "What are ye saying?"

"He killed the Highlander for his coin and his boat then dumped him in Abbey Wood." She sneered at Willis. "Then you came back to St. Bees and boasted about it, you heathen boy."

The blighter squirmed. "I'll burn you for this, you old crow."

Ian's knees buckled with the sick roiling in his gut. The bastard in his arms reared. Blinking, Ian reverted to fighting mode and jammed the knife harder. "I ought to slay the lot of ye!"

The crowd backed.

Bran and his men stepped forward, weapons ready for a fight. The cowardly onlookers scattered until the old woman and Willis were all that remained. Bran sheathed his sword. "We must collect Alexander's remains and take them to Brochel. Give him a proper burial."

It was all he could do not to run his blade across the murderer's exposed throat. Grinding his teeth, Ian restrained his urges and nodded toward his captive. "Tie his hands." He pressed his lips against Willis's ear. "If ye want to live, ye'll show us where ye dumped me brother." *Though I cannot say what I'll do once we arrive.*

***

Hands bound, Willis had been stomping around the wood far longer than it should have taken anyone to find a rotting corpse, and Ian was in no mood to allow him more time. Besides, the stench of death should still be sickly in the air. Ian's gut roiled with dread, his chest hollow. He hardened his mind to his own remorse. There was an ugly duty to perform, and he'd see it done. The time would come to mourn his loss once Alexander was laid to rest at Brochel Castle.

Ian kicked a stone. It rolled to a stop on an overgrown path. He crouched down and studied the tracks—human prints. Fresh ones. A thick canopy of trees sprung overhead, concealing it from passersby. "Where does the path lead?" he asked.

"Nothing that way. All of Abbey Wood is haunted." Shuddering, Willis pointed east. "They sacked the priory in the Reformation—killed all the monks."

Ian believed in ghosts about as much as he did bogles. "Come. This path has so many prints, 'tis obvious something lies to the south." He gave a grave nod to Bran. It may lead nowhere, but one thing was for certain…Alexander's body had been moved. Be the shift caused by animal or human was yet to be determined.

They hadn't hiked a mile when the path opened to a clearing with a cottage. A wee dog pressed his backside against the door and growled. One of Ian's men cocked his musket and pointed.

"No." Ian snatched a piece of bully beef from his sporran. Hand out, he moved forward. "There's a good laddie."

The odd-looking, liver-colored dog sniffed the beef and then licked. Ian didn't have time for niceties and tossed the dried meat aside. Wagging its tail, the dog dashed after it.

Ian knocked. "Hello?"

Nothing.

He tried the latch. When it clicked, he stepped inside. The place was neatly kept. The fire in the hearth had burnt to ash. A dirty shirt draped over a wooden chair caught his eye.

Bran must have seen it too, because he strode over and picked it up. "Could be his." He sniffed. "It has the laird's smell, too."

Pushed by a guard, Willis followed the floppy-eared dog through the doorway. "Mother Mary," he said with a hint of incredulity.

"What?" Ian asked.

"I didn't believe it when the town crier came by." He walked over and pointed to a crest above the mantel. "This is where Lady Whitehaven was hiding."

"Who?" Ian asked.

"She killed her husband." Willis glanced away. "The crier said two thiev—er…farmers from St. Bees found her, took her to Whitehaven to stand trial for murdering the earl."

This nightmare grows worse. Alexander was abducted by brigands and left for dead. Then his shirt ends up in the cottage of a murderess…a countess, no less. Ian paced, the damned dog keeping to his heel.

A Raasay guard pushed past the Englishman. "Someone camped in the stable, m'laird. There's a pallet and I found this."

Ian held out his hand. The guard rubbed his fingers and copper-colored beard shavings filled Ian's palm.

Alexander is no' dead.

Ian glared at Willis. "How far is it to Whitehaven?"

***

Jane spent a sleepless night shivering, crouched in the stone corner of the Whitehaven dungeon. Why had she allowed Alexander to walk out of her life? He had been so angry with her. Why had she been too afraid to tell him of her crimes—expose her vulnerability? What would he have done? Leave her alone in the wood? He'd gone and done that anyway—because she was a daft, selfish woman.

She never should have allowed Mr. Cox to hide her in Abbey Wood. She should have given herself up to the sheriff and faced her consequences. Jane hated hiding, living in fear, jumping at every sound from the forest. Existing tucked away in a hidden cottage was no life. She was a miserable failure. She couldn't cook a pottage without destroying the food. She bit her fist. Even Max sometimes turned his nose up at her cooking.

A tear streamed down her face. *Dear Lord, please protect Max. Help the poor little dog to find a new home and someone to care for him.*

A key scraped in the dungeon door then the hinges creaked open. Carrying a torch, only the outline of the guard was visible. "The Lord of Whitehaven wishes to see you. Come."

Jane braced her hands against the cold stone wall and stood. Why didn't they just execute her and have it done with? Must she endure humiliation by Roderick's cousin? Moving forward, she wiped her hands on her skirts and straightened her wimple as best she could.

Jane felt like a stranger walking through the cloisters of Buttermere Castle. She'd reigned as countess there for eight years, yet the halls seemed foreign, as if her prior life had never happened. Servants had made themselves scarce. She spied nary a one, not even Mr. Cox.

The guard took no chances. They marched in a diamond formation, one in the front, one in back and two at her flanks. *My, they must consider me quite dangerous. If only I had the skill to overpower them.* They led her directly to Roderick's solar—now John's, she reminded herself.

When the door opened, Lord John Drake stood facing the hearth, a goblet in his hand. From the rear, he presented an attractive form—tall with square shoulders, his blond hair neatly brushed and cropped to his nape. He wore a black velvet cape over one shoulder with matching breeches and hose. A cutlass rested in a scabbard at his hip.

"Lady Jane Drake, the Countess of Whitehaven," the guard announced.

John whipped around, his steely blue eyes boring into her. "Former countess." He sneered and sauntered up to her while the door closed behind.

Heart stuttering, her gaze darted from side to side. The door was the only way out, unless she attempted a leap from the second-story window. She hated how Drake men could belittle her with a look. Sickly fear churned in her stomach when their soulless eyes met hers.

Chuckling, he brushed a soft finger across her cheek. "Pretty Jane—unfortunate you have a murderous side." He tsked his tongue.

Her mouth growing dry, she inclined her head away from his touch.

He smirked. "Am I unappealing to you?"

She cast her gaze to the floor. Though attractive, his likeness to Roderick opened too many horrid memories. Jane's palms perspired. She inched toward the door. "You are agreeable, my lord."

He threw back his head and laughed—rather callous for a man who was about to pronounce her death sentence. "You always were the charming one, Jane." He examined his fingernails and then snapped his gaze back to her face. "Did you murder my cousin?"

She glanced over her shoulder and placed her hand on the latch.

"There's nowhere to run, dear Jane. Guards are posted outside the door." Trapping her, he placed his palms either side of Jane's head and leaned in. "Roderick had a penchant for the lash. Did he use it on you, dear one?"

"Please, my lord. I do not care to reminisce about my former husband's abuse."

"Aha." John's steely eyes widened. "I thought he may have pushed you too far. You never seemed like the murderous type."

His eyelids lowered and he gazed at her mouth. He leaned so near, Jane feared he would kiss her. "No!" She dipped under his arm and skittered around to the far side of the table. "I beg of you, do not toy with me. Issue my sentence and let it be done."

From across the room, his wolfish smile brought back the terror of that horrendous night. "What was it like plunging the knife into Roderick's flesh?"

Jane backed toward the wall. "Please stop."

"Let me help you." He sauntered toward her. Jane backed. He lunged like an asp, reached under her wimple and grasped a handful of hair. Jane ground her teeth against the searing pain of her tresses being pulled too taut. "Was he hurting you like this?" His free hand recoiled and he slapped her across the face.

Jane dropped to her knees. Pain radiated throughout her cheek. Her hand covered the burn. *Blood.*

"Did you spy the knife? Did you snatch it from his belt and plunge it into his soft flesh? What was it like, Jane? Did the blade slide in easily, or did you have to thrust and twist it in?"

"Stop this."

He yanked off her wimple and pulled her up by the hair. "'Tis a pity they didn't clean you up before they brought you to me." He held her against the wall and nuzzled her neck. Jane bit back her urge to scream.

"Marry me and I'll absolve you of your crimes."

She inclined her neck aside so he could see her eyes. Baring her teeth, she hissed. "Never."

He re-coiled for another slap. Jane ducked and wrenched from his grasp. Pushing chairs aside, she darted to the window. John grasped her waist and tugged. Jane held on to the sill and twisted with all her strength.

The door opened. "Beg your pardon, my lord," Mr. Cox said.

The earl tugged harder. "What the bloody hell do you want?"

"Excuse the interruption, but the sheriff has come to call."

With a heave, John pulled her from the window and touched his lips to Jane's ear. "Think about my offer. Things wouldn't be so awful with me. Though I'd never be as careless as my cousin." He pushed her toward Mr. Cox. "Have the guard take her away."

Moving through the passageways, Mr. Cox said nothing until he'd dismissed the guard and they were alone in the dungeon. "I'll see to it you have a pallet made up and proper food."

Jane nodded. "My thanks."

He wrung his hands. "My lady. I must say I overheard his proposal."

"No!" She threw her palms up and paced. "I'd rather die than live through an endless nightmare akin to the life I had with Roderick."

"But, my lady, it would at least purchase time."

"For what? Once I am married to John Drake, I'll be his property. If I were to flee, where would I go? What recourse would I have if he found me?"

"There's no other choice…"

Jane grasped his shoulders and shook. "I would rather meet my end. Can you not understand?"

"My lady." He gaped at her. "You are serious?"

"Yes." She clasped a hand to her throat, imagining it stretched in a noose.

"That's it, then." Mr. Cox's shoulders sagged. "May God have mercy on your soul. There is nothing more I can do for you."

Chapter Twelve

Three days of fishing in the Irish Sea not only had Alexander exhausted, every crew member on the English galley was dragging. The captain appeared to be the only lively soul on the boat, though Alex was certain the man had already counted the coin he expected to earn from the catch. The sailors all received an extra ration of ale on the journey home.

Alex manned an oar to assist their progress. With a heavy load and a single sail, the crew and galley needed all the power they could muster. His back ached and a nasty blister had burst on his palm, but that wasn't what worried him. Unfortunately, this task left him unable to scan the waters for *The Golden Sun*, though he figured his ship would be long gone by now.

When the galley approached Whitehaven, it was late afternoon. Alexander looked forward to payment for his share of the catch, a good meal and a perhaps a soft bed in the inn. If he was lucky, he might find someone who'd seen his ship and knew where it was heading.

"Hoist the oars," the captain hollered. "Prepare to dock and drop anchor."

Alexander rubbed his neck and pulled his oar in with the other sailors. He stretched and stood. "I'll be a monk of Judas," he mumbled under his breath. A seaman tossed him a rope. He caught it, but didn't avert his eyes from *The Golden Sun*. Ignoring the other crew members, he dropped the line and hopped onto the rowing bench. His gaze darted across the busy dockyard.

A sailor knocked him from his perch. "So now you're the king of the shite-eaters, are you, Highlander?"

"All hands," the captain bellowed. "No one will be paid until the galley is offloaded and the catch is recorded by the clerk."

Alexander brushed himself off and set to furling the sail. At least from that vantage point he could keep an eye on the pier. One head stood tall above the others—black, wavy hair touched broad shoulders. *Och aye, no one would miss Bran's beefy noddle in a crowd.*

Two sailors slid the gangway into place. Alexander didn't wait. He raced for the plank and bounded across it before they had a chance to secure the thing to the dock.

"Where the bloody hell do you think you're…" The captain's voice was swallowed up by distance and the noises of carts, horses and bartering merchants.

"Bran!" Alex yelled, sprinting for the shoreline. He'd lost sight of the head of black hair, but kept running. "Bran," he hollered again.

Rounding a cart piled with hay, Alexander nearly barreled into the big man's chest. Grasping Alex's shoulders, Bran braced him firmly. "Holy falcon feathers, did ye drift down from the heavens? We've been combing Whitehaven for days looking for ye, m'laird." Bran released his hands and gave Alex a hearty slap on the back.

Alexander coughed and returned the gesture with a firm fist in the arm. "Wheesht. I've been trying to earn me fare back to Raasay. Me boat was heisted by a pack of thieving E—" Alex glanced at the mob of Englishmen surrounding them. "By miserable thieves."

"I ken." Bran inclined his head toward the alehouse. "Ian's directing the search from inside the Ship Inn. We'll all want to hear yer story for certain."

As they approached the inn, Ian pushed out the big door. "Where on God's earth have ye been?"

Alexander and Ian clasped elbows in greeting and held firm. "For the past few days I've sailed the Irish Sea earning me wages as a paid seaman." Alexander clenched his jaw, choking back the excited flutter that swelled from his belly to his throat. By God, it was good to see his kin.

Ian twisted his face, a look he'd affected since childhood—one Alexander had oft teased him about. "What the devil were ye doing that for?"

Alex spread his palms to his sides. "I had to earn some coin to pay me fare home."

Bran clapped his shoulder and tugged him toward the inn. "What's it like to be a common hand?"

Alexander blew on his blistered palm. "Bloody hard work."

"Laird Alexander of Raasay, is it?" a man's voice trilled behind them.

Turning, Alexander knitted his brows. "Mr. Cox?"

"I've grave news." He gestured toward the door. "Only to be divulged in private."

"Is Lady—"

"Hush." Mr. Cox's stare darted back and forth across the scene. "Not here."

Alexander glanced at Ian. "Have you a room?"

His brother grasped the door latch. "Aye, follow me."

Hundreds of questions filled Alexander's head. The last time he'd seen Cox, the little man had practically run him out of Jane's cottage. Alex wanted to pick the bastard up and shake him. He could think of only one reason why the old fella would seek him out. *Something's happened. Something grave.*

Once above stairs, seeing the bed in the tiny chamber reminded Alexander he'd had little sleep in the past few days—but doubtless, rest would need to wait. As soon as the four men filed into the chamber and the door closed, Alex addressed Mr. Cox. "Where is Lady Jane?"

"Who?" Ian asked.

Alex sliced his hand through the air and kept his gaze focused on Cox.

"Taken." The little man shook his head and pressed the heels of his hands to his temples. "Not long after you left—someone must have seen you."

Alex reflected back to when he exited the forest. Indeed, a pair of crofters had pointed in his direction. "What of Jane? Where is she?"

Cox waved his thumb over his shoulder. "Buttermere Castle at the top of the hill—home of the Earl of Whitehaven."

Alexander didn't understand. "But is that not where she belongs?"

"She told you not?"

"I beg your pardon, but the lady divulged nary a secret."

"'Tis grave indeed, though now all of Whitehaven knows." Mr. Cox swiped a hand over his frown. "The former earl had a vile temper, and he oft beat his wife—our Lady Jane. As the earl's valet, I had no recourse but to sit in the nearby servant's quarters and listen to his frequent brutality."

Alexander's jaw twitched. He would never tolerate a man who sat idly by whilst a woman was being mistreated.

Cox gulped. "One night before Christmas, the argument grew worse than I'd ever heard. Lord Whitehaven was in his cups—angrier than a bull without a heifer. Noise of violence from the earl's chamber resounded through the walls. Lady Whitehaven pleaded with him to stop."

Mr. Cox rubbed his fingers over the hilt of the knife on his belt. "I pulled my dagger, ready to barrel through the servant's door, when everything went quiet. Pushing into the room, I found Lady Whitehaven standing over the earl's body with his blade in her trembling hands."

"And you spirited her to the cottage to hide her away from the sheriff," Alexander added.

"Yes—until a few days ago, when she was discovered by a seedy pair of louts from St. Bees." Mr. Cox looked him directly in the eye. "Unfortunately, the new Earl of Whitehaven is tarred with the same brush as his cousin."

"Jesus." Alexander combed his fingers through his hair. "Is Lady Jane all right?"

"Lord Drake is trying to force her to the altar. If she marries him, he'll absolve her of the accusation of murder."

"She cannot," Bran said. The big man didn't even know Jane, but the MacLeod henchman had as much tolerance for men who mistreated women as Alexander.

Cox shook his head with a grim frown. "She has refused him. I'm afraid our lady would rather face death than again live under the yoke of a tyrant."

Alexander turned to Bran. "I need a sword. How many fighting men do we have aboard *The Golden Sun*?"

"The tall ship in the harbor is yours?" Mr. Cox asked, clearly befuddled.

"Aye, and me cannons can blast this wee village out of England if we so desire."

Ian stepped in. "Is there any way to spirit her from Buttermere without inviting the earl's forces to give us chase?"

Mr. Cox rubbed the back of his neck. "He's locked her in the dungeon like a common criminal. You'd have to slip past the guard. That would be no easy feat."

Ian grinned. "Fortunately I've learned a thing or two from me lady wife. She's a healer."

Alexander liked the idea of storming the castle better. "Och, Ian. What if yer potion does no' work? Lady Jane is liable to meet her end. Every moment she remains within the walls of that castle, she's in danger."

"Can ye get us inside?" Bran asked.

Mr. Cox pursed his lips and regarded each man. "Dressed like Highlanders, you might be best to come in the back as if you're making a delivery to the kitchens."

Alexander's fingers itched for the feel of a claymore.

Grinning, Ian rubbed his palms together. "We could deliver a barrel of Raasay whisky laced with Merrin's nightshade—take it straight to the guardhouse."

Alex didn't like it. "Aye? And what do we do whilst we're waiting for the bastards to succumb to yer concoction?"

Ian chuckled. "A few drops of nightshade will work quickly—if it does no' kill the lot of them first."

"No, no." Cox waved his hands while shaking his head. "I do not want the death of a hundred soldiers on my hands."

"I was jesting. A few drops will no' kill them," Ian said. "But I guarantee they'll awake with a nasty pounding in their heads."

Bran looked at Alexander and crossed his arms. "I think 'tis our best option, m'laird. Gaining access through the servants' entrance—even if only half the guard drinks the whisky, I like our odds better than if we attack with cannons a blazing."

***

By the time they wheeled the cart with the barrel of whisky into Buttermere Castle's servants' entrance, Alexander had grown more confident with the plan. Besides Ian and Bran, it enabled them to smuggle in three more MacLeod fighting men, all wearing cloaks covering their heavy weaponry.

Mr. Cox led the procession across the courtyard, grinning from ear to ear. When they reached the guardhouse they were met by a disagreeable sentry holding a poleaxe. "State your business."

Cox gestured to the wagon. "There's a Scottish ship in port and they're peddling fine whisky. His lordship has arranged for a barrel in recognition of all the work you scruffy lot of guards have put in."

Alexander sized up the man. If the others were as beefy, they'd have a good fight for certain.

Beneath his helm, the guard scratched his head, looking as if he'd been thwacked between the eyes. "Lord Drake did that?"

"Yes." Cox directed the procession across the courtyard and into the guardhouse. "Why should he not? You've done a fine job in his eyes, mighty fine."

Alexander and the others offloaded the heavy barrel in front of the guardhouse door to block easy access. He turned full circle. The main gate was sealed shut by a portcullis, the cogs above on the next floor. At the side, a dimly lit passageway led into blackness—the route to the dungeon, no doubt.

Ian made show of removing the barrel's lid. "Ye'll find no better whisky than that from Highland stills…" There was no way they'd tell the bastards where the spirit had been distilled, else the Lord of Whitehaven might appeal to Queen Elizabeth's navy and wage a sea battle against Brochel Castle. While Ian and the others entertained the guard, Mr. Cox led Alexander through the passageway, retrieving a torch from the wall.

Cox fumbled with his keys. "She's in here."

Alexander peered through the tiny barred window in the door, but could see nothing. "Jane?" he whispered.

Once he'd slipped in the key, Mr. Cox turned it with a click. The door swung open. Alexander reached for the torch and strode inside. "Bloody hell." The chamber was empty.

"She must be with his lordship," Cox said.

"That raises the stakes in a deadly game." Alex panned across the chamber with the torch one more time. "Are ye certain they have no' taken her away from Buttermere?"

"Not since this morning." Cox gestured to the door. "Come."

Alexander replaced the torch on the wall before they came into view of the guardsmen. Bran shot him a questioning glance and Alex offered a subtle grimace.

"We'd best get back to the ship," Alexander said loudly so all could hear, then he inclined his head toward the inner bailey.

Once out of earshot of the guardhouse, Alexander faced the men. "Mr. Cox thinks she's with the earl." He pointed toward the back gate. "Wait for me by the kitchens. We'll no' get far if we all march up to the lord's chamber."

"Nay," Bran said. "Me laird isna heading into the lion's den without me sword to back him up."

"Or mine," Ian agreed.

One additional fighting man shouldn't cause alarm—but no more. Alex made a snap decision. "Bran, follow me. Ian, go with the guard. Your sword will be better served as we make our escape." Alexander nodded toward Mr. Cox. "Lead on."

Once inside, Jane's urgent voice echoed from the stairwell. Alex couldn't make out the words, but the high pitch and clipped sounds were unmistakable signs of treachery. Intense rage fired barbs of heat across his skin. His gut clenched with his urge to run—no room to push past Mr. Cox in the winding, narrow passage. "Faster!"

The valet hastened his step, though not quickly enough for Alex.

When they arrived on the third-floor landing, Alexander darted past him.

Two guards at the chamber door lowered their battleaxes in challenge.

Alexander raised his sword.

With a growl, Bran barreled ahead, his claymore hissing through the air.

Cox tugged Alex's arm. "There's a servants' entrance through the privy closet. Follow me."

Bran battled with both guards at once. "Go!"

A shriek sounded within the chamber, succeeded by a something scraping the floorboards. "You can do what you will with my body, but I shall *never* agree to marry you." God help him, it was Jane's voice.

"Quickly!" Alex fell in behind Mr. Cox, blood rushing in angry pulses beneath his skin. If he didn't get inside in the chamber within the blink of an eye, he'd hack his way through. Alexander shoved the old man in the back. "Ye'd best hasten faster, old man, else I'll move heaven and hell to break down that door."

The valet broke into a run. On his heels, Alex followed him through a narrow door leading into a dank passageway. A thud sounded. Jane screamed. Alexander could have leapt from his skin. Mr. Cox pushed through a wee door.

Alex ducked and barreled inside a cedar-paneled privy closet. In two steps, he clattered into the lord's chamber, bellowing his Highland battle cry. "Remove yer hands from me woman!"

Chapter Thirteen

Lord Drake clutched Jane's waist, his fingers digging into her flesh. Struggling, she twisted against his brutal grasp and slapped his face. He barely recoiled as his grip clamped harder.

The blackguard emitted a bone-chilling chuckle. "Yes, fight me, Jane. I like women with fire coursing through their blood." He hurled her onto the bed and flung up her skirts.

Jane rolled to her belly, scrambling to crawl across.

John gripped her legs with steely fingers and yanked her back. He crushed her with his body, whilst unlacing his breeches. With her skirts up around her knees, Jane struggled to writhe out from under him.

A clatter boomed from across the chamber. "Remove yer hands from me woman," a deep voice bellowed.

Alexander! Jane gasped, her heart fluttering from a wild rhythm of fear to a pummeling of hope.

Brandishing an enormous sword, he bounded inside. Watching the love of her life rush to her rescue filled Jane with renewed strength. She tore her wrists from John's grasp and forced her legs closed. "You shall never touch me like that again."

Reeling back, the earl drew his sword, spun and faced Alexander. "Guard," he hollered.

The door burst open. Two Whitehaven sentries slumped in the passageway with a hulking Highlander standing over them.

Alexander lunged.

John deflected the blow with an upward thrust.

The two men circled, crouched low, their gazes locked in a deadly stare.

Jane slid from the bed and pressed her body against the wall, frantically searching for a way to help Alexander. She snatched a candlestick from the bedside table and clutched it to her chest.

Mammoth sword in hand, the big Highlander from the passageway skirted toward her while Mr. Cox trembled, holding his dagger as if defending the privy closet.

The clang of swords rang out. Jane snapped her gaze toward Alexander and John.

The big Highlander grasped her arm. "Come, m'lady."

She tugged away. "I cannot."

With a nod, the man communicated his understanding. Shielding her with his body, he assumed a protective stance, holding his sword at the ready.

The earl swung his blade with deadly speed, driving Alexander toward the hearth. Alex defended the blows until he dipped under the attacking blade and spun, slicing his sword across the earl's side.

John howled and scooted away. "I'll see you bastards hang for this!"

Alex swung his sword in a circle. "And I'll see ye pay for mistreatment of Lady Jane." With the speed of a cat, he advanced, hacking with inhuman strength. John fought to deflect the blows, but his cutlass was no match for the two-handed sword. Baring his teeth, Alexander bore down with relentless vigor.

The earl backed into a chair. It toppled over with a clatter. He teetered and stumbled to his knees, dropping his cutlass. Alexander slid his blade against John's throat.

His lips quivering, the beaten earl looked a pathetic coward. "Spare me."

Alexander growled. "Give me one reason."

Jane stepped forward. "If you kill Roderick's cousin, I shall have the blood of two earls on my hands and will burn in hell for both crimes."

A shrill scream sounded from the corridor. "Guards, help! Our lord is under attack!" The chambermaid's footsteps resounded to the stairwell.

Jane cringed. "Please. We must flee."

With a growl, he slammed the pommel of his sword into John's temple. The earl dropped to the floor unconscious. Alex raced to Jane and pulled her into his embrace. "Are you all right, m'lady?"

"Yes, but…" Her candlestick clattered to the floor. "What are…? Where were…? How did…?"

Grinning, he silenced her mouth with a quick kiss. "I've no time to explain."

The big Highlander dashed to the door. "We'd best be gone afore any sober guards try to be heroes."

Alexander took Jane's hand and led her behind the black-haired warrior. "Bran will lead us out."

Mr. Cox hobbled behind them. "I'm afraid my tenure as the lord's valet has come to an end."

While they hustled down the stairwell, Jane squeezed Alexander's hand. "What did Bran mean by sober guards?"

He inclined his head toward her ear. "We delivered a barrel of whisky to the guardhouse, laced with a wee potion me brother concocted—something to make them sleep a day or two."

With no time to think about how the men might be adversely affected, Jane clung to Alexander's hand and followed him through the castle and out the big doors of the great hall.

They had nearly made it across the courtyard when Jane glanced over her shoulder.

"Stop them!" Blood streaking his face, John staggered toward the guardhouse. "Ride for the sheriff immediately, you slothful imbeciles."

As Jane and the men passed through the servants' gate, the last thing she heard was the creaking of the main portcullis. Horse hooves clomped over cobblestones. Evidently not everyone had succumbed to the brother's potion.

Joined by a small army of Highland warriors, Alexander pulled her outside the castle's curtain wall. "'Tis not far to the pier. Skiffs await us. Can ye run?"

She found enough breath to reply. "Yes." *How on earth does he think we can flee Whitehaven in a skiff?*

With no time to ask questions, Jane's legs burned as she ran behind the men all the way down Duke Street. She'd ridden to the pier many times, even walked the six town-blocks, but this passage seemed unending. Sucking in gasping breaths, she tried to keep up with the men's rapid pace. Her toe caught on a rock and she stumbled. Crying out, Jane flung her hands forward to break her fall.

Before she could stand, Alexander swept her into his arms. "Yer skirts are weighing ye down. I'll carry ye, m'lady."

As they neared the waterfront, horses rode into view and blocked their path to the wharf. Hisses filled the air as the Highlanders drew their swords. Bran moved in front of Alexander. "I'll cut a path for ye and the lady, m'laird."

Alexander slowed a tad to allow his men to advance. With inhuman bellows, the battle began. Jane clutched her arms around Alexander's neck and buried her face in his chest. Iron clashed with iron. Cannons blasted and whistled overhead. Jane's heart hammered. She clenched her eyes shut. *Is John firing from the battlements?*

More great thundering blasts sounded, shaking the ground. Jane dared look back. The volleys had come from the sea.

"Hold tight." Alexander sprinted through the throng.

Jane cringed when a sword whirred through the air a mere foot from her head.

The sound of Alexander's footfalls became hollow when he sprinted onto the wooden pier. Hoofs clattered behind.

"That's far enough, you pox-ridden whoreson," the Earl of Whitehaven bellowed.

Alexander glanced behind and sidestepped toward the slanted gangway of a galley. He set her beneath. "Wait here," he clipped.

Drawing his sword, he spun and faced the bloodied earl. With a hideous laugh, John spurred his horse to a gallop, cutlass held high. Alexander challenged him, his feet wide and planted firmly on the deck. With a swooping strike, the earl aimed for Alexander's head. Crouching, the laird spun outward. The earl's sword missed him by a hair.

Jane leaned forward on her hands and rolled to her knees. A pole teetered beneath her leg—*an oar.*

At the end of the pier, John reined his horse around. Rearing, the steed sped toward Alexander again. Jane tugged the oar, but it didn't budge. She rose to her feet and tried again, frantic to release it. Grinding her teeth, she bore down with all her weight. With a scrape, the oaken oar broke free. Spinning in place, she eyed Lord Drake, a name she loathed.

She used her momentum to swing the oar above Alexander's head. It slammed into John's chest. Upon impact, the makeshift weapon flew from her grasp. Reeling backward, Jane watched the earl's body topple from his horse and slam against the deck with a squelching thud. Unable to break her fall, she crashed to her back.

Alexander raced beside her. "My God, Jane, are ye hurt?"

She loved the sound of his voice when he spoke her name. Reaching up, she clasped his handsome face and drew his lips near. "I'm well enough to kiss you."

He crushed his mouth over hers. She threaded her fingers through the hair at his nape, reveling in the wildness of his taste. Jane's rugged Highlander had risked his life for her rescue and she would never again let him go. His tongue swirled while he gathered her in his arms. Her insides burst with a fluttering of joy.

Alexander sucked in a deep breath and stood, pulling her up by the elbows. "We must away to the skiffs afore we face another attack."

Behind them, iron clanged as the Highland warriors fought their way down the pier.

Alex dashed to a small boat tied at the end of the dock. "I'll step in and help ye aboard." He climbed into the little boat and stood firm. Looking up, he offered his hand. "M'lady."

She placed her palm in his. Rough fingers encased hers. "How do you expect to flee to the Highlands in this?"

Alexander chuckled and pointed to an enormous galleon at anchor in the harbor with sails unfurled. "These wee boats will serve to ferry us to me ship."

She clapped a hand over her mouth. "That grand galleon is yours?"

"Aye, *The Golden Sun*. Taken in battle by me father and passed to me upon his death."

By the time Jane settled upon a bench, Alexander's men had arrived, panting and bloodied.

"Launch the skiffs afore more English bastards can swing their puny swords at us," shouted a Highlander with flaxen hair. He clambered into the boat and took up an oar.

"That's me brother, Ian." Alexander moved to the bench beside Jane while the other men climbed aboard with Mr. Cox. "Ye must forgive his vulgar tongue. He's the one who mixed the potion."

Jane grinned at the handsome man—though not as ruggedly alluring as Alexander. "My thanks, sir knight." She looped her arm through the crook in Alexander's elbow and held him close. Over her shoulder, soldiers surrounded the earl. She stared at them until an excited yip resounded from the ship—Max's bark.

***

Clutching the rope for dear life, the crewmen winched Jane onto the deck. Three pairs of hands pulled her over the rail. "Welcome aboard, m'lady," said a rather spry sailor with a Highland burr she'd grown to adore.

"Thank you." Once on her feet, Jane quickly took in her surroundings. Ropes hung from the rigging, the sails billowed with the wind. The boat groaned as if begging to be set to sea. From the bow, Max yipped, his toenails tapping the deck as he ran to greet her. Jane clapped her hands. "Come here, boy!"

Max skidded to her, spun in a circle three times and jumped on her leg. Jane bent down and scrubbed her fingers into the dog's back. He slurped his tongue across her face. "Oh, you dear ragamuffin."

Alexander threw his leg over the rail. "He's mighty glad to see ye, m'lady."

"However did you find him?"

Ian bent down and patted Max's head. "He followed us from yer cottage."

"I shall be forever grateful that you took him in." Jane watched them pull Mr. Cox aboard from his perch on the winch.

A musket fired from the pier. With a jolt, Jane grasped Alexander's arm.

"We're nay out of this yet." He placed a firm and reassuring hand across her shoulders. "All hands man yer battle stations. Weigh anchor!"

"Aye, captain," the men brayed.

Jane clutched her fists under her chin. "Do you think they'll come after us?"

Alexander pointed. "Is that the sheriff on the pier?"

Squinting, Jane scarcely made out his red and gold tunic. "Yes, that is he."

Chains groaned and the ship swayed while it got underway toward the open sea. Alex grasped her hand. "Come with me."

He led her up to the quarterdeck at the bow of the ship and scanned the shore. "It looks as if the sheriff hasn't a warship at his disposal. I doubt we'll hear from them again, but a sea captain can nay tell his men to stand down when in enemy waters."

Jane marveled at the grandeur of Alexander's galleon. Decks clean and well maintained, it was as impressive a ship as she'd ever seen. She rested her hands on the rail. "I thought you would be long gone. How did you find me?"

The sun brought out a brilliant blue in Alexander's eyes, and he smoothed his fingers down her back. "Your Mr. Cox had something to do with it. I worked aboard a fishing galley for a few days, saw *The Golden Sun* anchored in the harbor when we returned with our catch…and then when I located me men, Mr. Cox appeared from the crowd and informed me of your plight."

"'Tis a miracle you were still in Whitehaven."

Alexander pressed his lips to her temple. "'Twas meant to be. For I cannot live without ye."

Jane closed her eyes and allowed herself to savor his words. Never in her life did she consider she would be happy sailing to the

Highlands on a grand ship, completely and utterly in love with a Scottish laird.

***

Alexander stood at the rail beside Jane and watched the shores of England fade, replaced by the verdant outline of the Scottish mainland. He laced his fingers through her exquisitely soft, fine-boned hands and nuzzled into her silken tresses. "I'm so overwhelmingly sorry for leaving ye in the wood."

"But you had to go." She pulled her hand away and stepped aside. "I acted selfishly. I was terrified to reveal my past because I was afraid. I am the one who should be asking for forgiveness."

"Nay." After all Jane had endured, he couldn't imagine her begging an apology from anyone. "Now that I know…"

"I need to tell you what happened. Like you said, love cannot grow between two people when dark secrets simmer beneath."

"There's no need." Alexander pulled her into his arms and breathed in the sultry scent of her tresses. "Ye were battered. Any man who raises a hand against a woman is a coward and deserves the gravest of punishments."

Her arms tightened around his waist. "But I took Roderick's life."

"Because he was attacking ye. If ye hadn't acted, he would have killed ye—I ken men like that. Sooner or later, ye would have ended up dead."

She kept her eyes downcast. "I know in my heart your words are true, but I took *his* life, not he mine. My actions were still wrong."

"I do no' believe it." He raised her chin with the crook of his finger and met her gaze. "I've killed in battle afore—this is no different. Every living soul has a God-given right to protect himself, be it lass or lad. Christ, Jane, ye cannot even bring yerself to kill a chicken. I do no' believe ye could ever take a life unless provoked to defend yerself."

She smiled, her eyes glistening with tears. "'Tis true. I cannot bear to harm any innocent creature."

"Ye see? Ye're the most kindhearted woman I've ever known."

She cupped his face in her palms. "I promise I will never keep anything from you again."

"Nor I you. I love ye, Jane."

Sultry as summer's heat, Jane rose up on her toes and Alexander met her lips with a low growl. She tasted of honey and pure woman. He drew her soft body against his chest, never wanting to release his hold. "Marry me."

"Yes." She ran a delicate finger over his lips. "I would spend the rest of my days with no other. I love you to the depths of my soul, Laird Alexander."

Books by Amy Jarecki:

Highland Force Series:

Captured by the Pirate Laird

The Highland Henchman

Beauty and the Barbarian

Return of the Highland Laird (A Highland Force Novella)

The Kings Outlaws series

Highland Warlord

Highland Raider

Highland Beast

Highland Defender Series

The Fearless Highlander

The Valiant Highlander

The Highlander's Iron Will (a novella)

Lords of the Highlands Series:

The Highland Duke

The Highland Commander

The Highland Guardian

The Highland Chieftain

The Highland Renegade

The Highland Earl

The Highland Rogue

The Highland Laird

Guardian of Scotland (Time Travel) Series

Rise of a Legend

In the Kingdom's Name

The Time Traveler's Christmas

Highland Dynasty Series:

Knight in Highland Armor

A Highland Knight's Desire

A Highland Knight to Remember

Highland Knight of Rapture

Highland Knight of Dreams (a novella)

Devilish Dukes Series:

The Duke's Fallen Angel

The Duke's Untamed Desire

The Duke's Privateer

Secret Longings of a Duke (a novella)

The MacGalloways series

A Duke, by Scot

Her Unconventional Earl

The Captain's Heiress

Kissing the Twin

A Princess in Plaid

Charmed by the Wily Lass

Blitzed series

Defenseless

Unintentional

Tackled

ICE Series (romantic suspense)

Hunt for Evil

Body Shot

Mach One

Pict/Roman Romances:

Rescued by the Celtic Warrior

Celtic Maid

Stand Alone Titles:
My Genes Don't Fit
Time Warriors
Defenseless
Virtue: A Cruise Dancer Romance
The Chihuahua Affair
Boy Man Chief

Visit Amy's web site and sign up for her newsletter:

www.amyjarecki.com